瑞蘭國際

瑞蘭國際

完全命中

領隊導遊
英文
考前衝刺

陳若慈　著

以輕鬆無痛的方式，
準備領隊導遊英文考試

　　不論是專攻領隊還是導遊，也不管外語是不是選擇英文這科，所有的考生都有其他3科（領隊／導遊實務（一）、領隊／導遊實務（二）、觀光資源概要）需要好好熟記，而且對大部分的考生來說，其他3科絕對要花最多心力與時間準備才能通透。然而從資料分析來看，領隊導遊考試的考生平均年齡多在40歲左右，且多半是有工作的上班族，要擠壓出時間唸書已屬不易，更何況共有4科要研讀，因此英文被分配到的時間可說是所剩無幾，所以如何以最少的時間掌握領隊導遊英文的重點，就是考生最在意的事情了。其實，領隊導遊英文與其他科目一樣，歷屆考題重複性高，只要能夠挑出最常出現的單字與句子詳加研讀，就能輕鬆搞定大部分的考題！

　　本書精選歷屆考題最常出現的16大情境，每一佳句都是從考題中挑選出來的，絕非憑空自擬，也因此在閱讀本書的同時，等於在熟悉歷屆考題題型。此外，本書更將歷屆考題打散，以相似的考題整併為同一情境，而非以零散的方式學習，不僅可以用最少的時間掌握重點，且能夠加深記憶。《完全命中！領隊導遊英文考前衝刺》對還沒做過考古題的考生而言，讀完本書後若有時間練習考古題，會大大地降低對考題的陌生與恐懼；而對已經練習過考古題的考生，閱讀本書時則得以將腦海中的考題，用清晰易懂的方式再整理過一回，加強應試功力。

本書的編排方式淺顯易懂，16大情境分類不一定要依序研讀，但每一單元建議先看完「單字」，再唸「佳句」；若時間允許，看完「佳句」之後，再看回「單字」，如此一來更能加深印象。在閱讀不同單元的過程當中，眼尖的讀者可能會發現句子內有越來越多眼熟的單字，佳句似乎也越來越簡單，那就表示讀者對於領隊導遊英文的理解程度也越高！希望這本書能夠帶給各種程度的讀者，以輕鬆「無痛」的方式準備領隊導遊英文！

陳若慈

關於專門職業及技術人員普通考試
導遊人員、領隊人員考試

簡單來說，本項考試就是為了取得導遊、領隊證照的考試。然而領隊、導遊考的科目各有不同，唯一相同的是兩者都會考「外語」這科。而《完全命中！領隊導遊英文考前衝刺》，就是為了這兩種應試類別中的科目——外語（英語）所撰寫的。

應考資格：

凡中華民國國民，具有下列資格之一者，即可應考：

一、公立或立案之私立高級中學或高級職業學校以上學校畢業，領有畢業證書或學位證書者。（同等學力者，須附教育部核發之同等學力及格證書）

二、初等考試或相當等級之特種考試及格，並曾任有關職務滿四年，有證明文件者。

三、高等或普通檢定考試及格者。

應試科目：

導遊人員考試分成「筆試」與「口試」二試，第一試「筆試」錄取者，才可以參加第二試「口試」。領隊人員考試則僅有「筆試」。

應試類別		應試科目	
		第一試（筆試）	第二試（口試）
導遊人員	外語導遊人員	1、導遊實務（一）：包括導覽解說、旅遊安全與緊急事件處理、觀光心理與行為、航空票務、急救常識、國際禮儀。 2、導遊實務（二）：包括觀光行政與法規、台灣地區與大陸地區人民關係條例、兩岸現況認識。 3、觀光資源概要：包括台灣歷史、台灣地理、觀光資源維護。 4、外國語：分英語、日語、法語、德語、西班牙語、韓語、泰語、阿拉伯語、俄語、義大利語、越南語、印尼語、馬來語等十三種，由應考人任選一種應試。	採外語個別口試，就應考人選考之外國語舉行個別口試，並依外語口試規則規定辦理。

應試類別		應試科目	
		第一試（筆試）	第二試（口試）
領隊人員	外語領隊人員	1、領隊實務（一）：包括領隊技巧、航空票務、急救常識、旅遊安全與緊急事件處理、國際禮儀。 2、領隊實務（二）：包括觀光法規、入出境相關法規、外匯常識、民法債編旅遊專節與國外定型化旅遊契約、台灣地區與大陸地區人民關係條例、兩岸現況認識。 3、觀光資源概要：包括世界歷史、世界地理、觀光資源維護。 4、外國語：分英語、日語、法語、德語、西班牙語等五種，由應考人任選一種應試。	不需口試。

※注意！應試科目均採測驗式試題，因此英語考試也都是四選一的選擇題，共計80題。

及格標準與成績計算方式：

一、外語導遊人員考試，筆試+口試平均加總成績滿60分為及格。

　　筆試：即為第一試，成績占75％（如上方表格外語導遊人員4科：導
　　　　　遊實務（一）＋導遊實務（二）＋觀光資源概要＋外語）。筆
　　　　　試成績滿60分為及格標準，依以上4科成績平均計算。但若筆
　　　　　試有一科為0分（缺考亦以0分計算），或外國語科目成績未滿
　　　　　50分，都不算及格，也不能參加口試。

　　口試：即為第二試，成績占25％。首先筆試（第一試）平均成績須達
　　　　　60分，才有資格參加口試。口試成績則須滿60分才及格。

　　　　簡單來説，也就是筆試成績須及格（滿60分），才有口試資格，
　　　口試也須滿60分，才會錄取。而其中任一科均不得缺考、或是0分，
　　　且外語筆試至少須達50分，整體才算及格。

二、外語領隊人員考試，筆試平均加總成績滿60分為及格。

　　　　以4科筆試成績平均計算（如上方表格外語領隊人員4科：領隊實
　　　務（一）＋領隊實務（二）＋觀光資源概要＋外語）。筆試成績平均

滿60分為及格標準，但若筆試有一科為0分（缺考亦以0分計算），或外國語科目成績未滿50分，都不算及格。

※注意！導遊、領隊考試平均考試成績須滿60分才算及格，但單就英語筆試這科，若未滿50分，即便其他科目再高分、平均成績有達60分，也不算及格！

資格取得：

一、考試及格人員，由考選部報請考試院發給考試及格證書，並函交通部觀光局查照。但外語導遊人員、外語領隊人員考試及格人員，應註明選試外國語言別。

二、前項考試及格人員，經交通部觀光局訓練合格，得申領執業證。

相關考試訊息：

測驗名稱：專門職業及技術人員普通考試導遊人員、領隊人員考試

測驗日期：每年3月（筆試）及5月（口試）

放榜日期：當年4月（筆試）及6月（口試）

等　　級：專技普考

測驗地點：分台北、桃園、新竹、台中、嘉義、台南、高雄、花蓮、台東、澎湖、金門、馬祖十二考區舉行。

報名時間：前一年11月開放報名

實施機構：考選部專技考試司

更多相關資料，請上考選部網站查詢。http://wwwc.moex.gov.tw

如何使用本書

→Step1，背誦「關鍵單字」和「嚴選佳句」

16大類重點情境

從歷屆試題中統整精選出16大類必考情境，按照情境記憶「關鍵單字」和「嚴選佳句」，讓你完全命中領隊導遊英文！

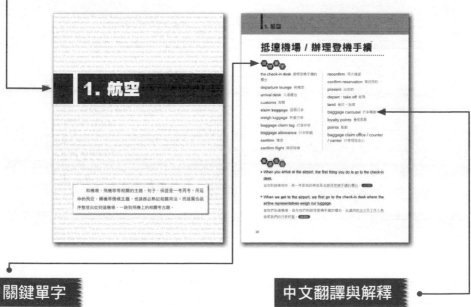

關鍵單字

每個情境下都有相關的重要單字，以情境來記憶關鍵單字，並同時列出相同意思的其他單字，讓你記得快、背得牢！

中文翻譯與解釋

精準的中文翻譯、相關說明與延伸解釋，讓你加深對單字的印象！

嚴選佳句

　　16大類中的佳句，每一句都是必考重點，來不及做考古題沒關係，只要多看幾次嚴選佳句，就能像做完數回考古題一樣的事半功倍！

補充 / 重點

　　嚴選佳句除了皆有精準的中文翻譯之外，對重點句子還會有補充的文法小教室，或是與句子相關的學習重點，讓你理解更快速、學習有效率！

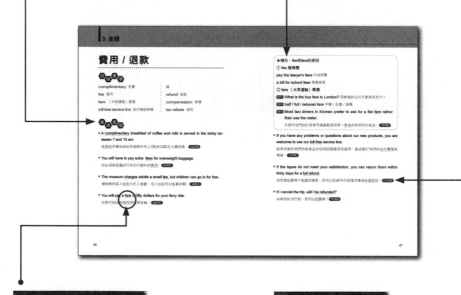

底線強調重點

　　每句嚴選佳句都有劃上底線，讓你一眼就能看出當句重點所在！

歷屆試題標示

　　每句嚴選佳句後面都有標上出自哪一個考試年度，而非作者自擬的考題，讓你對考題更有信心！

→Step2，考前背誦「黃金72小時重點單字卡」

黃金72小時重點單字卡

　　考前來不及看考古題了怎麼辦？這裡挑出關鍵單字精華中的精華，讓你只要沿著裁切線剪下，便可以隨身帶著背！另外，空白的地方也可以填上自己沒把握的單字，客製化屬於自己的「黃金72小時重點單字卡」！

附錄 黃金72小時重點單字卡			
A		**A**	
a must-see for visitors	必遊景點	aircraft、plane	飛機
a train / bus route	火車 / 公車路線	airplane	飛機、航空公司
absent	缺席的	airport security rules	機場安全規定
accommodation	住宿	airport	機場
adventure	冒險	aisle seat	靠走道的座位
affordable	買得起的	aliens	外國人
agenda	議程	alternative	其他的選擇
agreement	協議	amazing	令人驚豔的
ahead	事先	amenities	設施

11

目　錄

1. 航空

和機場、飛機等等相關的主題、句子，保證是一考再考。所延伸的飛安、轉機等情境主題，也請務必熟記相關用法。而這篇也依序整理出從到達機場，一路到飛機上的相關考古題。

抵達機場 / 辦理登機手續

the check-in desk 辦理登機手續的櫃台

departure lounge 候機室

arrival desk 入境櫃台

customs 海關

claim baggage 認領行李

weigh luggage 秤重行李

baggage claim tag 行李存根

baggage allowance 行李限額

confirm 確認

confirm flight 確認班機

reconfirm 再次確認

confirm reservation 確認預約

present 出席的

depart、take off 起飛

land 著陸、抵達

baggage carousel 行李轉盤

loyalty points 會員點數

points 點數

baggage claim office / counter / center 行李領取中心

▶ When you arrive at the airport, the first thing you do is go to the <u>check-in desk</u>.

當你到達機場時，第一件要做的事就是去辦理登機手續的櫃台。 100導遊

▶ When we get to the airport, we first go to the check-in desk where the <u>airline representatives</u> <u>weigh our luggage</u>.

當我們到達機場，首先我們到辦理登機手續的櫃台，此處的航空公司工作人員會將我們的行李秤重。 98導遊

▶ We arrived at the airport <u>in good time</u>, so we had plenty of time for checking in and boarding.

我們<u>及時</u>抵達機場,所以還有很多時間可以辦理報到手續及登機。 99領隊

▶ Even though you have <u>confirmed</u> your flight with the airline, you must still be present at the check-in desk on time.

即便你已經和航空公司<u>確認</u>班機,你還是必須準時到辦理登機手續的櫃台報到。 99導遊

▶ The flight is scheduled to <u>depart</u> at eleven o'clock tomorrow. You will have to get to the airport two hours <u>before the takeoff</u>.

班機預定於明天11點<u>起飛</u>。你必須在<u>起飛前</u>2個小時抵達機場。 99導遊

▶ Though most airlines ask their passengers to check in at the airport counter two hours <u>before the flight</u>, some international flights <u>require</u> their passengers to be at the airport three hours <u>before departure</u>.

雖然多數的航空公司<u>要求</u>乘客於<u>班機起飛前</u>2個小時到機場的櫃台登記,有些國際線班機還是<u>要求</u>乘客在<u>起飛前</u>3小時到達機場。 102導遊

▶ I was overjoyed to learn that I had accumulated enough <u>loyalty points</u> to upgrade myself from <u>coach</u> to business class.

我感到超級開心,因為我已經累積足夠的<u>會員點數</u>讓我從<u>普通艙</u>升級到商務艙。 101領隊

▶ Tourist: What is the <u>baggage allowance</u>?
Airline clerk: It is 20 kilograms per person.

<u>旅客</u>:<u>行李的限額</u>是多少?
<u>航空公司職員</u>:每個人20公斤。 101領隊

▶ As a general rule, checked baggage such as golf clubs in golf bags, serfboards, baby strollers, and child car seats are not placed on a <u>baggage carousel</u>.

一般來說，託運行李像是高爾夫球俱樂部的高爾夫球袋、衝浪板、嬰兒推車以及兒童汽車安全座椅不會被放在<u>行李轉盤</u>上。 `100導遊`

證件

pick up 領取

boarding pass 登機證

passport 護照

identification 證件

get on / get off airplane 上 / 下飛

機

expiry date 到期日

expire 過期

entry permit 入境許可證

visa 簽證（申請passport或是visa

▶ Now you can purchase a seat and pick up your <u>boarding pass</u> at the airport on the day of departure by simply showing appropriate <u>identification</u>.

現在你可以買票（購買座位），並且於出發當天在機場只出示適當<u>證件</u>來領取<u>登機證</u>。 101領隊

▶ A <u>boarding pass</u> is a necessary document for the passenger to get on the airplane.

<u>登機證</u>是乘客登機的必要文件。 99導遊

▶ You will get a <u>boarding pass</u> after completing the check-in.

在完成登機報到手續之後，你將會拿到一張<u>登機證</u>。 98領隊

▶ People traveling to a foreign country may need to <u>apply for a visa</u>.

人們到國外旅行可能需要<u>申請簽證</u>。 98領隊

▶ You must check the <u>expiry</u> date of your passport. You may need to <u>apply</u> for a new one.

你必須檢查你的護照的<u>到期</u>日。你也許需要<u>申請</u>一本新的。 `100領隊`

▶ If you're travelling to the United States, you may need a <u>visa</u>.

如果你到美國旅行,你可能需要<u>簽證</u>。 `100領隊`

▶ He got his visa <u>at the eleventh hour</u>.

他在<u>最後一刻</u>拿到簽證。 `98領隊`

▶ When traveling in a foreign country, we need to <u>carry</u> with us several important documents at all times. One of them is our passport together with the <u>entry permit</u> if that has been so <u>required</u>.

當在外國旅遊,我們需要隨身<u>攜帶</u>幾份重要的文件。如果<u>被要求</u>的話,其中一項就是我們的護照和<u>入境許可證</u>。 `102導遊`

安全檢查 / 飛安相關

leave the ground 起飛

on board、in flight 飛機上

flight safety 飛行安全

security check 安全檢查

airport security rules 機場安全規
定

result in 導致

search 搜查

carry 攜帶

carry-on bags 隨身行李

prohibited items 違禁品

ban 禁止

examine、inspect 檢查，兩者都
為檢查之意，但inspect更有「權力」

▶ Before the plane <u>leaves the ground</u>, we must watch a video related to <u>flight safety</u>.

在飛機起飛前，我們必須觀看和飛安有關的影片。 100領隊

▶ <u>Disobeying the airport security rules</u> will result in a civil penalty.

違反機場安全規定會導致民法的刑責。 101領隊

▶ Please <u>examine</u> your luggage carefully before leaving. At the <u>security counter</u>, every item in the luggage has to go through <u>inspection</u>.

在出發前請仔細檢查你的行李。在安檢櫃台時，行李內的每一項物品都會被檢
查。 99導遊

21

▶ In the interests of safety, passengers should <u>carry</u> neither dangerous items nor matches while on board.

為了安全考量，乘客不能<u>帶</u>危險物品或是火柴登機。 `101領隊`

> ⚠ 重點：in the interests of 因為……的考量。

▶ For safety reasons, radios, CD players, and mobile phones are <u>banned on board</u>, and they must remain <u>switched off</u> until the aircraft has <u>landed</u>.

由於安全的因素，收音機、CD播放器、手機都<u>禁止在飛機上使用</u>，且必須保持<u>關機</u>的狀態直到飛機<u>降落</u>。 `101領隊`

▶ If you carry keys, knives, aerosol cans, etc., in your pocket when you pass through the security at the airport, you may <u>set off</u> the alarm, and then the airport personnel will come to <u>search</u> you.

當你通過機場的安檢區時，如果你帶著鑰匙、小刀、噴霧罐等東西在你的口袋，你可能會<u>引發</u>警報器，接著機場的人員會來<u>搜查</u>你。 `101領隊`

▶ <u>Prohibited items</u> in <u>carry-on bags</u> will be confiscated at the checkpoints, and no <u>compensation</u> will be given for them.

<u>隨身行李</u>中的<u>違禁品</u>將會於檢查站被沒收，且沒有任何的<u>補償</u>。 `101領隊`

▶ All passengers shall go through <u>security check</u> before boarding.

登機前所有乘客都應該通過<u>安全檢查</u>。 `98領隊`

▶ Beware of strangers at the airport and do not leave your luggage <u>unattended</u>.

小心機場的陌生人，不要讓你的行李<u>無人看管（在視線之外）</u>。 `98領隊`

> ⚠ 重點：國外常見告示牌寫Please do not leave personal belongings unattended.
> 請勿讓隨身行李無人看管。

海關 / 移民局

immigration officer 移民官

hesitate 猶豫

customs 海關

customs officers 海關官員

aliens 外國人

import 進口

deport 驅逐出境

passport control 護照審查管理處

clear customs 結關、清關或者通關，指進口貨物、出口貨物和轉運貨物時，進入一國海關關境或國境必須向海關申報，辦理海關規定的各項手續

▶ When answering questions of the <u>immigration officer</u>, it is advisable to be straight forward and not <u>hesitating</u>.

當回答<u>移民官</u>的問題時，建議<u>實話實説</u>，並且不要<u>猶豫</u>。 102導遊

▶ <u>Customs officers</u> usually have a <u>stern</u>-looking face and they have the right to ask us to open our baggage for <u>searching</u>.

<u>海關官員</u>通常看起來很<u>嚴肅</u>，而且他們有權利為了<u>搜查</u>的目的而要求我們打開行李。 102導遊

▶ The man at the <u>passport control</u> did not seem to like the photo in my passport, but in the end he let me through.

在<u>護照審查管理處</u>的人似乎不喜歡我的護照照片，但最後還是讓我通過了。 101導遊

▸ It took us no time to <u>clear customs at the border</u>.

<u>於邊界通關</u>沒有花我們什麼時間。 102領隊

▸ <u>Aliens</u> who overstay their visas would be <u>deported</u> back to their country of birth.

逗留得超過簽證規定時間的<u>外國人</u>會被<u>驅逐出境</u>送回他們的出生國家。 102領隊

▸ Each country has its own <u>regulations</u> regarding fruit and vegetable <u>imports</u>.

關於水果與蔬菜的<u>進口</u>，每個國家都有其<u>規定</u>。 101領隊

登機前廣播

require 需要

boarding gate 登機門

final boarding call、
last call for boarding、
final call announcement、final
call 最後登機廣播

▶ "Good evening, ladies and gentlemen. This is the <u>pre-boarding announcement</u> for flight 67B to Vancouver. We are now inviting those passengers with small children, and any passenger <u>requiring</u> special assistance, to begin boarding at this time. Please have your boarding pass and identification ready. Regular boarding will begin in <u>approximately</u> ten minutes. Thank you."

「大家晚安，各位先生女士們。這是飛往溫哥華的67B班機的<u>登機前廣播</u>。我們現在先請帶小孩、或是<u>需要</u>特別協助的乘客現在開始登機。請準備好您的登機證以及證件。一般乘客登機<u>約</u>將於10分鐘後開始。謝謝。」 98導遊

▶ This is the <u>final boarding call</u> for China Airline Flight 009 to Hong Kong at Gate C2.

這是飛往香港的中華航空009班機於C2登機門的<u>最後登機廣播</u>。 102導遊

▶ In some airports, there is the <u>final call announcement</u>, but in others, they only have blinking signals on the sign board. Passengers are responsible for their own arriving at the boarding gate in time.

某些機場有<u>最後登機廣播</u>，但有些只有告示牌上一閃一閃的訊號。乘客必須自行負責及時到達登機門。 102導遊

▶ Didn't you hear the <u>final call</u>? Come on, we need to go now or we'll miss our flight.

你沒有聽到<u>最後登機廣播</u>嗎？快點！我們要現在過去不然就會錯過班機了。

100導遊

機組人員

flight attendant 空服員

stewardess 空姐

steward 空少

cabin crew 機組人員

captain 機長

▶ On my flight to Tokyo, I asked a <u>flight attendant</u> to bring me an extra pillow.

在前往東京的班機，我要求<u>空服員</u>給我額外的枕頭。 101導遊

▶ <u>Flight attendants</u> help passengers find thelr seats and <u>stow</u> their carry-on luggage safely in the overhead compartments.

<u>空服員</u>幫忙乘客找到座位，並且幫助他們將隨身行李安全地<u>放</u>於頭頂上的置物箱內。 99導遊

座位相關

window seat 靠窗的座位　　　　　middle seat 中間的座位

aisle seat 靠走道的座位

▶ Please check your ticket and <u>make sure</u> that you are sitting in the correct seat.

請檢查你的票並確定你坐在正確的座位上。 `100導遊`

⚠ 重點：make sure 確定。

▶ When I <u>take a flight</u>, I always ask for an <u>aisle</u> seat, so it is easier for me to get up and walk around.

當我搭飛機時，我總是要求靠走道的座位，這讓我比較容易起身走動。 `98導遊`

飛行中

cruise 飛行、航行

turbulence 亂流

fasten 繫緊

seat belt 安全帶

on board 在飛機上

touch down 著陸

taxi in 飛機在航道上滑行

get off an airplane / a bus / a train 下飛機 / 巴士 / 火車

get on an airplane / a bus / a train 上飛機 / 巴士 / 火車

▶ The airplane is <u>cruising</u> at an altitude of 30,000 feet at 700 kilometers per hour.

飛機目前以每小時700公里的速度，<u>航行</u>於30,000英尺的海拔上。 98領隊

▶ Airliners now <u>cruise</u> the ocean at great speed.

飛機目前以高速來越洋<u>飛行</u>。 98領隊

▶ I was very scared when our flight was passing through <u>turbulence</u> from the nearby storm.

當飛機通過來自附近暴風雨的<u>亂流</u>時，我真是嚇壞了。 101導遊

★ 補充：機上遇到亂流時，經常會廣播以下注意事項。

例句 "We are approaching some turbulence. For your safety, please keep your belts fastened until the 'seat belt' sign goes off."

「我們正接近某個亂流。為了您的安全，請繫緊安全帶直到『座位安全帶』的指示燈熄滅。」101領隊

例句 Please keep your seat belt fastened during the flight for safety.

為了安全，飛行途中請繫緊您的安全帶。98領隊

★ 補充：buckle up 繫好（安全帶）

例句 My father always asks everyone in the car to buckle up for safety, no matter how short the ride is.

不管路程多短，為了安全著想，我爸爸總是要求車上每個人都繫好安全帶。101領隊

⚠ 重點：buckle up = fasten seat belt 繫好安全帶。

▶ Please remain seated while the plane takes off.

當飛機起飛時，請保持就坐。99領隊

▶ I found myself on board an airplane.

我發現我自己在飛機上。100領隊

▶ After the plane touches down, we have to remain in our seats until we taxi in to the gate.

飛機降落後，我們必須待在座位上，直到滑入登機口。100領隊

▶ When you are ready to <u>get off an airplane</u>, you will be told not to forget your personal <u>belongings</u>.

當你已經準備<u>下</u>飛機時，你將會被告知別忘了帶走你的隨身<u>物品</u>。 99導遊

▶ During <u>take-off</u> and <u>landing</u>, carry-on baggage must be placed in the overhead compartments or underneath the seat in front of you.

在飛機<u>起飛</u>和<u>降落</u>其間，隨身行李都必須放置於頭頂上的置物箱內，或是在你前面的座位底下。 101領隊

轉機

direct flight 直飛班機

transfer 轉機

connecting flight 轉機班機

stopover 中途停留

▶ Passengers <u>transferring</u> to other airlines should report to the information desk on the second floor.

要<u>轉</u>搭其他班機的乘客請到2樓的櫃台報到。 101領隊

▶ Client: Are there any <u>direct flights</u> to Paris?

Clerk: No, you would have to <u>transfer</u> in Amsterdam.

客人：有到巴黎的<u>直飛班機</u>嗎？

服務員：沒有，你必須到阿姆斯特丹<u>轉機</u>。 102領隊

▶ The flight will make a <u>stopover</u> in Paris for two hours.

飛機將<u>中途停留</u>巴黎2個小時。 101領隊

▶ <u>Due to the delay</u>, we are not able to catch up with our <u>connecting flight</u>.

<u>因為延遲</u>，我們無法趕上我們的<u>轉機班機</u>。 102領隊

班機延誤 / 取消

delay 延誤

divert 轉向

stormy weather 暴風雨的天氣

inclement weather 惡劣的天氣

impending 即將發生的、逼近的

disaster 災害、災難

due to 因為

▶ There was a slight departure <u>delay</u> at the airport due to <u>inclement</u> weather outside.

因為外面惡劣的天氣，機場班機起飛有些延誤。 100領隊

▶ Our flight was <u>diverted</u> to Los Angeles <u>due to</u> the stormy weather in Long Beach.

因為長灘的暴風雨，我們的班機被迫轉向到洛杉磯。 101領隊

⚠ 重點：diverted 被轉向。stormy weather = inclement weather 惡劣的天氣。

▶ The airlines could have explained to us about the <u>long flight delay</u>, but they just kept us waiting and did not say anything.

航空公司大可以向我們解釋班機嚴重延誤的原因，但他們只是讓我們等，什麼也不說。 102導遊

33

1. 航空

▶ "Flight AB123 to Tokyo has been <u>delayed</u>. Please <u>check</u> the monitor for <u>further</u> information about your departure time."

「飛往東京的AB123班機已延誤了。請查看螢幕上進一步關於起飛時間的訊息。」 98導遊

> ⚠ 重點：check有各類的用法，考生請務必牢記。此處的check為查看、確認，check亦可作為帳單。check-in則為登機手續。

▶ As the flight to the Bahamas was <u>delayed</u> for eight hours, all passengers were <u>going bananas</u>.

由於飛往巴哈馬的班機延誤8小時，所有乘客都快氣瘋了。 98領隊

▶ Due to the <u>impending disaster</u>, we have to <u>cancel</u> our flight to Bangkok.

因為即將到來的災害，我們必須取消到曼谷的航班。 100領隊

▶ Due to the delay, we are not able to <u>catch up with</u> our connecting flight.

因為延遲，我們無法趕上我們的轉機班機。 102領隊

★補充：postpone和delay的不同

① postpone 延期，一般指有安排的延遲，常說明延到什麼時候。

例句 If the rain doesn't stop soon, we should consider <u>postponing</u> Joe's farewell party.

如果雨再不停，我們應該考慮延期喬的歡送派對。 100導遊

例句 The meeting has been <u>postponed</u> to next Monday.

會議延到下星期一。

② delay 延遲，常表示由於外界的原因而拖延。

例句 The storm <u>delayed</u> the flight. 班機因暴風雨延遲。

準備降落 / 下飛機

▸ After <u>disembarking the flight</u>, I went directly to the <u>baggage claim</u> to pick up my bags and trunks.

<u>下飛機</u>後，我直接走向<u>行李認領</u>處拿我的包包和行李箱。 101領隊

⚠ 重點：常考單字為baggage claim 行李認領。

motorcar in the early 20th century. Railway companies in Europe and the United States used streamlined tra
933 for high-speed services with an average speed of up to 130 km/h (80 mph) and a top speed of more than 1
100 mph). The first high-speed train was the Italian ETR 200 that in July 1939 went from Milan to Florence at 1
with a top speed of 203 km/h. With this service, these trains were able to compete with the upcoming airplanes.
the Odakyu Electric Railway in Greater Tokyo launched its Romancecar 3000 SSE. This set a world record
gauge trains at 145 km/h (90 mph), giving Japanese designers confidence that they could safely build even fas
at standard gauge. Desperate for transport solutions due to overloaded trains between Tokyo and Osaka, the idea
peed rail was born in Japan. There is no globally accepted standard separating high-speed rail from conventio
ds; however, a number of widely accepted variables have been acknowledged by the industry in recent yea
lly, high-speed rail is defined as having a top speed in regular use of over 200 km/h (125 mph). A tour manager
ual duties to perform to run a tour smoothly and successfully. For instance, the tour manager should always be
e up every morning in order to make sure each team member is ready before the bus leaves for the next scenic s

2. 交通

ms, such as stolen passports, physical ailments and medical emergencies. Most importantly, the tour manager m
e group members home safe and sound at the end of the journey and get ready for the next trip. Recently, a n
f tourism, or what is called 'alternative tourism', has emerged and become more and more popular among peop
el tired of the same old holidays and hope to gain real or authentic experiences from traveling. This new kind
n takes the form of individual custom-made or independent holidays that take people to remote and exo
tions, and cater to their different needs and interests. These holidays are basically designed and arranged a
al level. They often have different themes and offer a variety for people to choose from. As the market for this n
f tourism has expanded greatly, newer topics and programs will also appear as long as people begin to devel
interests and needs in the future. But what exactly can people get out of alternative tourism? For ecology-mind
, they can go whale-watching or take a conservation trip to help restore the damaged coastline. For people who l
ure and outdoor activities, the choices could range from mountain climbing, scuba diving, windsurfing, white-wa
to cycling in the mountains and deserts. For people who simply like to relax and gain a peace of mind, they c
a week at spa and health resorts to relax and de-stress, or take yoga and meditation lessons at country retreats
For people who are fond of culture and heritage, they can visit museums and art galleries in New York, take
nd break at the Edinburgh International Festival, or tour around France to visit historic castles. Other progra
alternative tourism include holidays that are taken for educational, artistic or religious purposes. These conta

　　不論是帶團，或是自助旅行，在旅途中一定會遇到各類型的交通英文，只要了解基本的單字，便能輕鬆了解題意。而這些單字除了考試之外，實際旅遊上也非常實用，快納入自己的口袋吧！

y. Railway companies in Europe and the United States used streamlined trains since 1933 for high-speed servic
average speed of up to 130 km/h (80 mph) and a top speed of more than 160 km/h (100 mph). The first high-spe
was the Italian ETR 200 that in July 1939 went from Milan to Florence at 165 km/h, with a top speed of 203 km
is service, these trains were able to compete with the upcoming airplanes. In 1957, the Odakyu Electric Railway
Tokyo launched its Romancecar 3000 SSE. This set a world record for narrow gauge trains at 145 km/h (90
Japanese designers confidence that they could safely build even faster trains at standard gauge. Desperate

2. 交通

關鍵單字

transportation vehicles 交通工具

maintain 維護

leave for、head to 前往某處

leave 離開

express 快的、直達的、快車

set route 固定的路線

itinerary 旅程、路線

destination 目的地

charter bus 遊覽車

shuttle service 接駁巴士服務

zone 地帶、地區

instruction 命令、指示

guarantee 保證

insert into 插入

get on 上車

嚴選佳句

▶ All transportation vehicles should be well-maintained and kept in good running condition.

所有的交通工具都該有完善的維護，且保持良好的運作狀態。 98領隊

▶ This express train leaves at 9:30 am every day. You can plan a short walk before that in the itinerary.

這班快車每天9點半出發。在那行程之前，你可以計劃散個步。 99領隊

▶ When a train arrives, the first thing you need to do is to check if its destination matches with where you want to go before you step in.

當火車到站，在你踏進車廂前，你需要做的第一件事就是確認目的地是否相符。

102導遊

▶ A bus used for public transportation runs a <u>set route</u>; however, a <u>charter</u> <u>bus</u> travels at the direction of the person or organization that hires it.

用來當大眾運輸工具的巴士有固定的路線，然而，<u>承租的巴士（遊覽車）</u>依照租車的人或團體來行駛。 `101領隊`

▶ I called to ask about the schedule of the buses <u>heading to</u> Kaoshiung.

我打電話過來問關於<u>開往</u>高雄的巴士時刻表。 `101領隊`

▶ Some cities do not have <u>passenger loading zones</u>. It is advisable to follow the instruction of the tourist guide to get off or get on the tour bus to <u>guarantee</u> safety and comfort.

有些城市沒有<u>乘客上下車的指定地方</u>。因此建議遵照遊客指南的指示上下觀光巴士，確保安全以及舒適。 `102導遊`

▶ Our hotel provides free <u>shuttle service</u> to the airport every day.

我們飯店每天免費提供到機場的<u>接駁巴士</u>服務。 `99領隊`

> ⚠ 重點：THSR Shuttle Bus 台灣高鐵接駁巴士，如從車站至機場兩點固定來回的，即稱shuttle bus。

▶ To use a TravelPass, you have to <u>insert</u> it <u>into</u> the automatic stamping machine when you <u>get off</u>.

要用旅遊通，當你<u>下車</u>時，你必須將票<u>插入</u>自動剪票機。 `99領隊`

▶ The driver has made a <u>request</u> that you throw all your garbage in the bin at the front on your way out.

這位駕駛<u>要求</u>你們下車時將垃圾丟入前方的桶子內。 `98導遊`

> ⚠ 重點：made a request也可作為ask，都為要求別人。

▶ A: "Excuse me. Can I take this seat?"

B: "Sorry, it is occupied."

A：「抱歉。我可以坐這個位子嗎？」

B：「抱歉，這座位有人坐。」 101導遊

⚠ 重點：位子有人坐有2種常見説法，The seat is occupied / taken.而詢問位子是否有人坐，則可以説：Is this seat taken?

3. 金錢

不可否認的，出門在外就是需要金錢！而此單元除了旅人常見到的換匯、退款等花費議題外，也包含經濟概況，甚至是個人理財、花費等，都是常見考題。請務必把握這大類的單字！

個人花費 / 購物

cash 現金

credit card 信用卡

traveler's check 旅行支票

exchange rate 匯率

foreign currency 外幣

withdraw 提領

deposit 存入

savings account 儲蓄存款戶頭

surcharge 附加費用

transaction 交易

refrain from 避免，有忍住、抑制之意

unnecessary 不需要的

necessary 需要的

stuff 物品、東西

budget 動詞為控制預算，名詞為預算

bargain 好價錢

A bargain is a bargain. 說話要算數。

bargain-hunting 四處覓購便宜貨

currency exchange、
money changing、
exchange money 換匯

denomination 面額，In what denominations? 要什麼面額的？

charge 名詞為費用，動詞為收費，

▶ You can get cash from another country at the <u>currency exchange</u> at the airport.

你可以在機場的<u>換匯櫃台</u>拿到其他國家的現金。 100導遊

▶ Money changing can be complicated. When in doubt, always ask some-one who is knowledgeable .

換匯可以是非常複雜的。當有疑慮時，請問了解的人。 102導遊

▶ We don't recommend exchanging your money at the hotel because you won't get fair rate.

我們不建議你在飯店兌換你的錢，因為你不會有公平的匯率。 99領隊

▶ May I have two hundred U.S. dollars in small denominations?

我可以兌換200美元的小額鈔票嗎？ 98領隊

▶ Client: I would like to change 500 US dollars into NT dollars.
   Bank clerk: Certainly, sir. Please complete this form and make sure you put the full name in capitals.

客戶：我想要將500美元換成新台幣。
銀行行員：沒問題，先生。請填此表格並且確保用大寫寫全名。 100領隊

▶ I would like to withdraw $500 from my savings account.

我想從我的儲蓄帳戶內提500元。 98領隊

▶ This traveler's check is not good because it should require two signatures by the user.

旅行支票不好用是因為它需要持有者的2份簽名。 102領隊

▶ I would like to charge this to my American Express card, please.

我希望可以用我的美國運通卡付費，麻煩了。 102領隊

▶ I'm afraid your credit card has already expired. Would you like to pay in cash instead?

恐怕你的信用卡已經過期了。你希望改以付現代替嗎？ 99領隊

▶ When you charge a foreign purchase to a bank credit card, such as MasterCard or Visa, all you lose with most cards is the 1 percent the issuer charges for the actual exchange.

當你用信用卡支付國外購物，像是MasterCard卡或是Visa卡，簽帳購物的損失是發卡銀行多收實際消費的1%。 98領隊

▶ Other banks, however , add a surcharge of 2 to 3 percent on transactions in foreign currencies. Even with a surcharge, you generally lose less with a credit card than with currency or traveler's checks.

然而，其他銀行於外幣交易時則加收2-3%的附加費用。即便有附加費用，相較於付現或是旅行支票，信用卡的損失還是比較少。 98領隊

▶ Therefore, don't use traveler's checks as your primary means of foreign payment. But do take along a few $20 checks or bills to exchange at retail for those last minute or unexpected needs.

所以不要以旅行支票當成國外付款的主要工具。但還是要準備幾張20元面額的支票或鈔票零用，以便最後一刻或是臨時購物之需。 98領隊

▶ The easiest way to look for the shop that you want to visit in a shopping center is to go to the directory or information desk when you fail to find out the answer from passers-by.

要在購物中心找到想要逛的店家，當你問路人得不到答案時，最簡單的方式就是走到導覽區或是櫃台。 102導遊

▶ A <u>boutique</u> is simply another name for a small <u>specialty</u> shop.

精品店也表示是賣<u>特殊</u>紀念品的小商店。 102導遊

▶ Sara bought a beautiful dress in a in a fashionable <u>boutique</u> district in Milan.

莎拉在米蘭的流行時尚區的一間<u>精品店</u>買了一件漂亮的洋裝。 101導遊

▶ To <u>save</u> money, buy just what you need and <u>refrain from</u> buying <u>unnecessary stuff</u>.

為了<u>省錢</u>，只買你需要的東西，且<u>克制不買</u><u>不需要的東西</u>。 99導遊

▶ Parents should teach their children to <u>budget</u> their money at an early age. Otherwise, when they grow up, they will not know how to manage their money.

父母應該在孩子還小時就教導他們如何<u>控制花費</u>。否則當小孩長大時，將不知如何理財。 98導遊

▶ If you want to find the cheapest aIrplane ticket, <u>bargains</u> can usually be found through the Internet.

如果你想要找最便宜的機票，通常可以在網路上找到<u>好價錢</u>。 99導遊

▶ All drinks served on the airplane are <u>complimentary</u>.

所有在飛機上所供應的飲料都是<u>免費的</u>。 98領隊

費用 / 退款

關鍵單字

complimentary 免費

fee 費用

fare （大眾運輸）票價

toll-free service line 免付費服務專

線

refund 退款

compensation 補償

tax rebate 退稅

嚴選佳句

▶ A complimentary breakfast of coffee and rolls is served in the lobby between 7 and 10 am.

免費的早餐有咖啡和捲餅於早上7點到10點在大廳供應。 102領隊

▶ You will have to pay extra fees for overweight baggage.

你必須替超重的行李支付額外的費用。 98領隊

▶ The museum charges adults a small fee, but children can go in for free.

博物館向成人收取少許入場費，但小孩則可以免費參觀。 98導遊

▶ You will pay a fare of fifty dollars for your ferry ride.

你要付50元的費用來搭乘渡輪。 98領隊

★補充：fee和fare的差別

① fee 服務費

pay the lawyer's fees 付律師費

a bill for school fees 學費帳單

② fare （大眾運輸）票價

例句 What is the bus fare to London? 到倫敦的公共汽車費是多少？

例句 half / full / reduced fare 半價 / 全價 / 減價

例句 Most taxi drivers in Kinmen prefer to ask for a flat fare rather than use the meter.

大部分金門的計程車司機喜歡使用單一費率而非使用計程表。 100導遊

▶ If you have any problems or questions about our new products, you are welcome to use our toll-free service line.

如果你對於我們的新產品有任何的困難或是疑問，歡迎撥打我們的免付費服務專線。 98領隊

▶ If the tapes do not meet your satisfaction, you can return them within thirty days for a full refund.

如果這些膠帶不能讓你滿意，你可以在30天內退還並獲得全額退款。 101領隊

▶ If I cancel the trip, will I be refunded?

如果我取消行程，我可以退費嗎？ 100領隊

★補充：refund

人之於refund（退費）為被動，refund此處為動詞，亦可為名詞，如：

例句 The guest is given a <u>refund</u> after he makes a complaint to the restaurant.

這名客人在他向餐廳抱怨之後拿到退款（名詞）。 99領隊

▶ Am I <u>entitled</u> to <u>compensation</u> if my ferry is canceled?

如果我的遊輪行程被取消了，我有權力要求補償嗎？ 102領隊

▶ If you have the receipts for the goods you have purchased, you can claim a <u>tax rebate</u> at the airport upon departure.

如果你有購物收據，離境時可於機場要求退稅。 98領隊

經濟 / 貿易

overlook 忽略

impact 衝擊

inflation 通貨膨脹

economic slowdown 經濟趨緩

economic prosperity 經濟繁榮

economic uncertainty 經濟不確定性

booming growth 蓬勃成長

boost the economy 振興經濟

economic recession 經濟蕭條

revenue 稅收

economic trauma 經濟創傷

bail out 保釋、紓困

international trade 國際貿易

surge 激增

decline、decrease 下降、減少

fine 處以……罰金

litter 亂扔廢棄物

spur domestic consumption 刺激國內消費

▶ Because of its inexpensive yet high-quality medical services, medical tourism is <u>booming</u> in Taiwan.

因為價格不貴又高品質的醫療服務，台灣的醫療觀光正蓬勃發展中。 `98導遊`

⚠ 重點：booming為景氣好的，而另一常見的blooming（開花），常用於興隆、興盛之意，如a blooming business 興隆的事業。

▶ Government officials have <u>overlooked</u> the impact of <u>inflation</u> on the economy.

政府官員忽略了<u>通貨膨脹</u>對經濟的影響。 `98領隊`

3. 金錢

▶ There is no denying that much of the world is still mired in an <u>economic slowdown</u>, but some of the brightest examples of significant and lasting opportunity are right under our nose.

不可否認的，世界大部分都深陷於<u>經濟趨緩</u>的狀況下，但其實有一些最棒以及持續的機會正在我們的眼前。 102導遊

▶ Thanks to India's <u>economic prosperity</u> and the <u>booming growth</u> of its airline industry, more Indians are flying today than ever before.

歸功於印度的<u>經濟繁榮</u>，以及該國航空業的<u>大幅成長</u>，如今有更多印度人搭飛機。 101導遊

▶ Tourism has helped <u>boost the economy</u> for many countries, and brought in considerable revenues.

旅遊業在許多國家已經幫忙<u>振興經濟</u>，且帶來可觀的收入。 99領隊

▶ The $3,600 shopping voucher program was designed to <u>spur domestic consumption</u>, and for most people, these vouchers are really "gifts from heaven."

3,600元的消費券是設計來<u>刺激國內消費</u>的方案，對於大多數的人來說，這些消費券真的是「天上掉下來的禮物」。 98導遊

▶ The depth of the current <u>economic trauma</u> is one that the ordinary Irish man or woman has found hard to accept, let alone fully comprenend.

目前<u>經濟創傷</u>的深度，達到一般愛爾蘭人難以接受的程度，更別說要充分瞭解了。 100導遊

▶ In time of <u>economic recession</u>, many small companies will <u>downsize</u> their operation.

在<u>經濟不景氣</u>時期，很多小公司都會<u>縮減</u>他們的經營。 98領隊

▶ The American government has decided to provide financial assistance to bail out the automobile industry. Car makers are relieved at the news.

美國政府決定提供財務援助來紓困汽車工業。汽車業者對此新聞感到欣慰。

`98領隊`

▶ International trade allows countries to buy what they need from other countries.

國際貿易讓各個國家可以向其他國家購買所需的東西。 `99導遊`

▶ Many emerging countries are facing economic uncertainty after the breaking up with former union.

很多新興國家自從與前聯盟瓦解後，都面對經濟的不確定性。 `102領隊`

★補充：break的片語

break 打破，以下許多片語請牢記：break up 打碎、分手、瓦解；break down 停止運轉；break into 破門而入；break through 突破。

▶ Since the economy is improving, many people are hoping for a raise in salary in the coming year.

既然經濟已經好轉，許多人希望明年能加薪。 `99領隊`

★補充：文法小教室

rise、raise、arise都有升起的意思，但各有不同：

① rise（rose, risen）是非及物動詞，其後不可有受詞。

例句 The sun always rises in the east. 太陽從東方升起。

② raise（raised, raised）是及物動詞，必須接受詞。

例句 Please raise your hand if you know the answer. 如果你知道答案，請舉手。

例句 The company will <u>raise</u> salaries by 5%. 公司將<u>加</u>薪５％。

例句 Many concerns were <u>raised</u> about South Africa hosting the World Cup in 2010, but in the end South Africa pulled it off and did an excellent job.

對於南非舉辦2010世界盃的疑慮<u>升高</u>，但最後南非消除了這些疑慮且表現出色。 101導遊

③ arise是非及物動詞，其後不可有受詞，常指事情的發生。

arise from / out of...即「由……造成」。

例句 Accidents always <u>arise from</u> the carelessness.

許多事故都<u>源於</u>粗心。 99領隊

▶ Although the <u>unemployment rate</u> reached an all-time high in mid-2009, it has fallen for four <u>consecutive</u> months by December.

雖然<u>失業率</u>於2009年年中一直都很高，但到12月時已經<u>連續</u>下降4個月。

99領隊

⚠ 重點：unemployment 失業；reach 抵達、伸手及到、達到，在此指達到。

其他

▶ By 2050, Africa's population, both northern and sub-Saharan, is expected to <u>surge</u> from 900 million to almost two billion.

到了2050年，非洲的人口，包含北非和撒哈拉沙漠，預計會從9億激增至20億。 100導遊

▶ We have seen a marked <u>increase</u> in the number of visitors to the theme park, but cannot understand why the total income indicates a <u>decline</u>.

我們看到主題樂園的遊客數已有顯著的<u>增加</u>，但卻不懂為何總收入卻<u>下滑</u>。 102領隊

⚠ 重點：decline、decrease都是下降、減少的意思。

▶ Our company has been on a very tight <u>budget</u> since 2008.

自從2008年，我們公司的<u>預算</u>就很緊縮。 99領隊

▶ You will be <u>fined</u> for littering in public places.

在公共場所亂丟垃圾會被<u>罰錢</u>。 98領隊

⚠ 重點：fine 處以……罰金；litter 亂扔廢棄物。國外路邊常見的標示Do not litter、No littering都是不要隨意丟棄的意思。

4. 旅程 / 旅行

此分類包含各式各樣旅遊相關的情境以及詞彙，非常生活化，除了考試之外，旅行時也很實用！以下精選的考古題例句都相當簡單，請務必把握得分關鍵！

旅遊趨勢

view as 把……當作是
（= regard... as）

affordable 提供得起的、買得起的

development 發展

necessity 必需品

luxury 奢侈品

ecotourism 生態旅遊

exotic 異國情調的

reward 獎賞

rewarding 有價值的

domestic 國內的

domestic flight 國內航班

international 國外的

international flight 國際航班

prosperity 興旺、繁榮

infrastructure 公共建設

impact 影響

▶ For many, vacations and travel are increasingly being viewed as a rather <u>necessity</u> than a <u>luxury</u> and this is reflected in tourist numbers.

對許多人來說，度假和旅行漸漸被視為一種必需品而非奢侈品，由旅遊人數可看得出來。 `101導遊`

▶ The <u>developments</u> of technology and transport infrastructure have made many types of tourism more <u>affordable</u>.

科技以及交通建設的發展，讓許多型態的旅遊更使人能夠負擔得起。 `101導遊`

▶ <u>Ecotourism</u> is not only entertaining and <u>exotic</u>; it is also highly educational and <u>rewarding</u>.

<u>生態旅遊</u>不只富有娛樂性和具有<u>異國情調</u>，更有高度教育性和<u>有價值的</u>。

101領隊

▶ The prosperity of <u>domestic</u> tourism is related to the <u>policy</u> of our government.

<u>國內旅遊業</u>的興盛與我們政府的<u>政策</u>有關。 100領隊

▶ Increasing tourism <u>infrastructure</u> to <u>meet</u> domestic and international <u>demands</u> has raised concerns about the <u>impact</u> on Taiwan's natural environment.

增加旅遊業的<u>公共建設</u>來<u>滿足</u>國內外的<u>需求</u>，對於台灣的自然環境而言已經有所影響。 102導遊

▶ The number of independent travelers <u>has risen</u> steadily since the new policy was <u>announced</u>.

因為新政策的頒布，自助旅行者的人數不斷地<u>增加</u>。 99領隊

※rise的詳細用法請見P.51。

實用知識

step out 踏出

inquire 詢問

accommodation 住宿

route 路線、路程

a train / bus route 火車 / 公車路線

map 地圖

brochure 小冊子

wireless internet access 無線網

路

chart 圖表

available 可得到的

unavailable 不可得的

appreciate 欣賞

draw attention to 引起對……的注意

take caution 注意

plunge into 跳入、投入

▶ Before you <u>step out</u> for a foreign trip, you should <u>inquire</u> about the accommodations, climate, and culture of the country you are visiting.

在你踏出國外旅程之前,你應該先詢問有關那個國家的住宿、天氣和文化。

101領隊

▶ Before taking a bus, it is advisable to check out its <u>route</u> on a computer or read carefully the <u>route chart</u> at the bus stop.

在搭公車之前,建議先在電腦上查明路線,或是在公車站時仔細閱讀路線圖。

102導遊

▸ All the routes on the city rail map are color-coded so that a traveler knows which direction she/he should take.

城市鐵路地圖的所有路線用顏色區分，這樣旅人才知道他們要搭哪個方向。
99領隊

▸ Don't over pack when you travel because you can always acquire new goods along the way.

旅行時不用打包太多東西，因為你總是可以在旅途中取得新物品。 101導遊

▸ As a general rule, it's best to avoid wearing white clothing and accessories when traveling. Go with darker colors that hide dirt well.

一般而言，外出旅行時最好避免穿白色衣服及配件。深色服裝比較能夠隱藏汙漬。 101導遊

▸ At the Welcome Center, you will find plenty of resources, including maps, brochures, and wireless internet access.

在迎賓中心，你可以發現很多資源，包含地圖、小冊子，以及無線網路。
101導遊

▸ Go to the office at the Tourist Information Center and they will give you a brochure about sightseeing.

去旅遊中心，他們會給你一本觀光手冊。 99領隊

▸ City maps are always available at the local tourist information center.

城市地圖可在當地旅遊中心取得。 98領隊

▸ In order to appreciate the architecture of the building, you really need to get off the bus and get closer to it.

為了欣賞建築物的結構，你真的需要下車，並靠它近一點。 98導遊

▶ Travelers should <u>familiarize</u> themselves with their destinations, both to get the most enjoyment out of the visit and to <u>avoid known dangers</u>.

旅客應<u>熟悉</u>所前往的目的地,可以享受觀光外也能<u>避免已知的危險</u>。 〔98導遊〕

▶ Watch out for your own safety! Don't be a target of <u>thieves</u> while you are traveling.

注意你的安全!當你旅遊時別成為<u>小偷</u>的目標! 〔99導遊〕

▶ Do not <u>draw attention</u> to yourself by <u>displaying</u> large amounts of cash or expensive jewelry.

不要藉由<u>展示</u>大量的錢和貴重首飾,來<u>引起</u>別人對自己的<u>注意力</u>。 〔100領隊〕

▶ The heavy rain in the valley often <u>affects</u> my <u>sight</u>, so I sometimes have to pull my car over to the side of the road and wait until the rain stops.

山谷內的大雨經常<u>影響</u>我的<u>視線</u>,所以有時候我必須停在路邊等雨停。 〔101導遊〕

▶ Motorists are strongly advised to <u>take caution</u> when they drive along windy mountainous roads to avoid plunging into a <u>ravine</u>.

強烈告誡摩托車騎士當行經風很大的山路時,要特別<u>注意</u>避免<u>墜入深谷</u>。 〔100導遊〕

▶ Be sure to dress warmly when <u>hiking</u> in the mountains. It gets cold in the afternoon.

當在山中<u>健行</u>時,記得穿得保暖。下午會變冷。 〔99導遊〕

計劃假期

package holiday 套裝行程

itinerary 行程（具有詳細計畫的含意）

journey 旅程

tour 旅遊

excursion 遠足

ahead 事先

in advance 事先

nail down dates 敲定日期

high season 旺季

equator 赤道

contingency plan 備案

pricey 貴的

It is high time 正是應該……的時候、是……的時候了

▶ If you take a package holiday, all your transport, accommodation, and even meals and excursions will be taken care of.

如果你選擇套裝行程，你所有的交通、住宿甚至餐食、旅遊都會被打點好。

99領隊

▶ Some tourists like to make plans and reservations for local tours after they have arrived. They prefer not to have every day of their vacation planned ahead.

有些觀光客喜歡在抵達目的地後，才安排當地的旅遊計畫以及預約相關事宜。他們不喜歡事先安排好假期的每一天的計畫。 98導遊

▶ Cindy and her husband are so busy that it is difficult for them to <u>nail down</u> dates for a vacation.

辛蒂與她的丈夫是如此地忙碌以至於很難<u>敲定</u>去度假的日期。 `100導遊`

▶ <u>It is high time</u> to talk about travel as the holiday season is now beginning in most countries north of the equator.

隨著北半球大部分國家的假期到來，<u>差不多是該</u>討論旅行<u>的時候了</u>。 `100導遊`

▶ The manager gave a copy of his <u>itinerary</u> to his secretary and asked her to arrange some business meetings for him during his stay in Sydney.

經理交給他的祕書一份<u>旅行計畫（行程）</u>，並且要求她幫他在雪梨的停留期間安排一些業務會議。 `101領隊`

▶ Your detailed <u>itinerary</u> is as follows: leaving Taipei on the 14th of June and arriving at Tokyo on the same day at noon.

你詳細的<u>行程</u>如下：6月14日離開台北，當天中午抵達東京。 `102領隊`

▶ Do they have a <u>contingency plan</u> if it rains tomorrow and they can't go hiking?

如果明天下雨他們不能健行的話，他們有<u>緊急備案</u>嗎？ `102領隊`

▶ The <u>downside</u> of touring in this city is that it's very <u>pricey</u>.

這座城市觀光的<u>缺點</u>就是<u>物價昂貴</u>。 `102領隊`

旅遊活動

leisurely 悠閒地

wander 漫遊、閒逛

take [have, go for] a stroll 散步、漫步

safari 狩獵遠征

adventure 冒險

cruise ship 載客長途航行的遊輪

uninhabited 無人居住的、杳無人跡的

guided tour 有導遊的遊覽

hiking 健行

savor 細細回味

▶ Susan Manning's trip to Buffalo was a/an leisurely one. She took her time.

蘇珊‧曼寧去水牛城的旅程是悠閒的。她從容不迫地度過她的時間。 [99導遊]

▶ I just spent a relaxing afternoon taking a stroll along the river-walk.

我剛剛沿著河邊散步，度過了一個悠閒的下午。 [101導遊]

▶ I love to go wandering; often I take my bicycle to tour around the country-side on weekends.

我喜歡閒逛，我週末常常騎腳踏車到鄉間旅行。 [102導遊]

▶ His one ambition in life was to go on safari to Kenya to photograph lions and tigers.

他畢生的雄心之一就是到肯亞狩獵遠征，拍攝獅子和老虎。 [100導遊]

▶ Exploring the culture and history of Africa sounds like a great <u>adventure</u>. It will be a lot of fun!

探索非洲的文化和歷史聽起來是個很偉大的<u>冒險</u>。這將會很有意思！ `99導遊`

▶ They <u>cruised</u> all around the Mediterranean for eight weeks last summer and <u>stopped off</u> at a number of uninhabited islands.

他們去年夏天<u>航遊</u>地中海8週，並在一些無人島上<u>停留</u>。 `100導遊`

※cruise亦作飛行，詳見P.29

▶ Our <u>guided tour</u> around the farm <u>lasted</u> for two and a half hours.

我們的農場<u>導覽</u>共持續2個半小時。 `99領隊`

▶ The <u>hiking</u> route of the Shitoushan Trail is not <u>steep</u> and so is suitable for most people, including <u>the elderly</u> and young children.

獅頭山步道的<u>健行</u>路線不太<u>陡峭</u>，所以適合大多數的人，包含<u>老人</u>和小孩。 `100導遊`

▶ <u>Whenever</u> there is a holiday, we always <u>go hiking</u>.

<u>無論何時</u>有假，我們總是<u>去健行</u>。 `100領隊`

▶ Even though John has returned from Bali for two weeks, he is still <u>savoring</u> the memories of his holidays.

即便約翰已經從峇里島回來2個星期了，他仍然對他的假期回憶<u>念念不忘</u>。 `102領隊`

motorcar in the early 20th century. Railway companies in Europe and the United States used streamlined tr
1933 for high-speed services with an average speed of up to 130 km/h (80 mph) and a top speed of more than
(100 mph). The first high-speed train was the Italian ETR 200 that in July 1939 went from Milan to Florence at
with a top speed of 203 km/h. With this service, these trains were able to compete with the upcoming airplanes
the Odakyu Electric Railway in Greater Tokyo launched its Romancecar 3000 SSE. This set a world record
w gauge trains at 145 km/h (90 mph), giving Japanese designers confidence that they could safely build even fa
at standard gauge. Desperate for transport solutions due to overloaded trains between Tokyo and Osaka, the ide
-peed rail was born in Japan. There is no globally accepted standard separating high-speed rail from conventio
ds; however, a number of widely accepted variables have been acknowledged by the industry in recent ye
ally, high-speed rail is defined as having a top speed in regular use of over 200 km/h (125 mph). A tour manager
dual duties to perform to run a tour smoothly and successfully. For instance, the tour manager should always be
ne up every morning in order to make sure each team member is ready before the bus leaves for the next scenic s

5. 旅遊景點

ms, such as stolen passports, physical ailments and medical emergencies. Most importantly, the tour manager n
e group members home safe and sound at the end of the journey and get ready for the next trip. Recently, a n
f tourism, or what is called 'alternative tourism', has emerged and become more and more popular among peo
el tired of the same old holidays and hope to gain real or authentic experiences from traveling. This new kind
m takes the form of individual custom-made or independent holidays that take people to remote and exc
ations, and cater to their different needs and interests. These holidays are basically designed and arranged a
al level. They often have different themes and offer a variety for people to choose from. As the market for this n
f tourism has expanded greatly, newer topics and programs will also appear as long as people begin to deve
interests and needs in the future. But what exactly can people get out of alternative tourism? For ecology-mind
, they can go whale-watching or take a conservation trip to help restore the damaged coastline. For people who l
ure and outdoor activities, the choices could range from mountain climbing, scuba diving, windsurfing, white-wa
to cyc

　　領隊的職責之一，便是介紹國外觀光景點。因此博物館、歷史遺跡、壯麗風景等相關的英文，絕對得熟記！除了書本之外，建議也可經常瀏覽國外各大旅遊網站，如TripAdvisor等旅遊評論網站，可得知國外各大城市以及景點名稱。在準備考試期間，不但能欣賞吸引人的旅遊相片，還能藉此學習相關英文，對於旅遊景點這類的考題，絕對大有幫助！

average speed of up to 130 km/h (80 mph) and a top speed of more than 160 km/h (100 mph). The first high-
as the Italian ETR 200 that in July 1939 went from Milan to Florence at 165 km/h, with a top speed of 203 km
his service, these trains were able to compete with the upcoming airplanes. In 1957, the Odakyu Electric Railway
r Tokyo launched its Romancecar 3000 SSE. This set a world record for narrow gauge trains at 145 km/h (90 mp
Japanese designers confidence that they could safely build even faster trains at standard gauge. Desperate

關鍵單字

exotic 異國風情的	cuisine 美食
foreign 國外的、陌生的	contrast 對比
foreigner 外國人	bursting with 充滿
site 地點、場所、網站	visually impaired 視障的
historic site 歷史遺址	physically impaired 殘障的
tourism 觀光業	auction 拍賣
tourist 觀光客	compete with 比得上
tourist destination 觀光景點	headquarters 總部、總公司
resort 名勝	demand 需要、要求
The Statue of Liberty 自由女神像	established （被）建立
island 島嶼	operate 運作、運轉
casino 賭場	secluded 隱蔽的、僻靜的
temple 廟宇	photogenic 上相的
palace 皇宮	be steeped in 充滿著、沉浸於
National Palace Museum 故宮博物院	fascinate 使神魂顛倒
concert hall 音樂廳	enigmatic 謎樣的
museum 博物館	enigma 謎
secluded beache 隱密性海灘	cascade 疊層成瀑布落下
scenic waterfall 美景瀑布	breath-taking 令人屏息的
peak 山頂	amazing 令人驚豔的
capital 首都	thrilling 令人興奮的
	spectacular 壯觀的、壯麗的

landscape 風景、景色

path 小徑、小路

meander 蜿蜒而流

wonders of the world 世界奇景

charming 迷人的

known for、famous for、
well know for 知名

remarkably 引人注目地、明顯
地、非常地

▶ Thailand is a pleasure for the senses. Tourists come from around the world to visit the nation's gold-adorned temples and sample its delicious cuisine.

泰國是個讓人感官感到愉悅的地方。來自世界各地的觀光客來拜訪此國家以黃金裝飾的廟宇，以及品嚐美食。 102導遊

▶ The Philippines is a country with more than 7,000 islands and it has dozens of native languages. What is even more amazing is the contrast between the north and the south, particularly their people's religious belief and political conviction.

菲律賓是一個有著超過7,000座島嶼，且有幾十種方言的國家。更令人驚訝的是南北方的對比，特別是人們的宗教信仰和政治理念都不一樣。 102導遊

▶ Paris' Cultural Calendar may be bursting with fairs, salons and auctions, but nothing can quite compete with the Biennale des Antiquaires.

巴黎的文化節目可能有展覽、講座和拍賣會，但沒有一個可以和巴黎古董雙年展相比。 102導遊

▶ Macau, a small city west of Hong Kong, has turned itself into a casino headquarters in the East. Its economy now depends very much on tourists and visitors whose number is more than double that of the local population.

澳門，位於香港西邊的小城市，現在已成為東方的<u>賭場</u>總部。其經濟仰賴比當地<u>人口</u>多上兩倍的觀光客。 `102導遊`

▶ Strictly speaking, Venice is now more of a <u>tourism</u> city than a maritime business city.

嚴格來說，威尼斯比較像<u>觀光</u>城市而不是海洋的商業城市。 `102導遊`

▶ I like Rome very much because it has many <u>historic sites</u> and it is friendly to visitors.

我非常喜歡羅馬，因為它有很多<u>歷史遺跡</u>，對遊客也很友善。 `102導遊`

▶ Kyoto is my <u>favorite</u> city because I prefer traditional Japanese culture to electronic culture.

京都是我<u>最喜歡</u>的城市，因為我喜歡傳統的日本文化更勝電子文化。 `102導遊`

▶ A single visit to Rome is not enough. The city's layered complexity <u>demands</u> time.

只去一次羅馬是不夠的。這座城市具有各種面向的複雜度<u>需要</u>時間瞭解。
`101導遊`

▶ <u>Established</u> in 1730, Lancaster's Central Market is the oldest continuously operating farmers market in the United States.

<u>設立</u>於1730年，蘭卡斯特中央市場是美國一直持續營運最老的農夫市場。
`101導遊`

▶ High in the mountains of Chiapas, San Cristóbal del la Casas is one of the most <u>photogenic</u> spots in Mexico: colorful, historic, and remarkably complex.

聖克裏斯多佛古堡位於契亞帕斯山上，是墨西哥最<u>適於拍照</u>的旅遊景點之一，多采多姿，有歷史意義，並且非常複雜。 `101導遊`

► With its <u>palaces</u>, sculptured parks, concert halls, and museums, Vienna is a <u>steeped</u> city in cultures.

有<u>皇宮</u>、用雕刻裝飾的公園、音樂廳和博物館，維也納是一座<u>充滿</u>文化的城市。 `101導遊`

► The oldest of all the main Hawaiian islands, Kauai is <u>known</u> for its <u>secluded beaches, scenic waterfalls, and jungle hikes</u>.

身為夏威夷群島最古老的島嶼，考艾島以<u>隱密性海灘、美景瀑布與叢林健走</u> 聞名。 `101導遊`

► The <u>Statue</u> of Liberty, a gift from France, is <u>erected</u> in New York Harbor.

自由女神<u>像</u>，是來自法國的禮物，<u>豎立</u>在紐約港。 `100領隊`

► Although there is more than one Paris in the world, there's really only one Paris in the world. It is the <u>capital</u> of France.

雖然全世界有一個以上名叫巴黎的地方，但是世界上其實只有一個巴黎。那就是<u>法國的首都</u>。 `100領隊`

► For centuries, artists, historians, and tourlsts have been <u>fascinated</u> by Mona Lisa's <u>enigmatic</u> smile.

數個世紀以來，藝術家、歷史學家，以及觀光客都對蒙娜麗莎謎樣般的微笑<u>深深著迷</u>。 `99導遊`

► Hong Kong is one of the world's most <u>thrilling</u> Chinese New Year travel destinations. The <u>highlight</u> is the spectacular fireworks display on the second day of the New Year.

香港是世界上<u>最令人興奮的</u>中國新年旅遊景點之一。<u>最精彩的部分</u>是大年初二壯觀的煙火表演。 `100導遊`

5. 旅遊景點

▶ The amusement park is a famous <u>tourist attraction</u> in Japan. Tourists of all ages love to go there.

這座遊樂園是日本很有名的<u>觀光景點</u>。各年齡層的觀光客都喜歡去那邊。
`99導遊`

▶ This <u>monument</u> <u>honors</u> the men and women who died during the war.

此<u>紀念碑</u>是為了<u>榮耀</u>在戰爭期間陣亡的男男女女。 `98導遊`

▶ The <u>results</u> of the New Seven Wonders of the World campaign were <u>announced</u> on July 7th, 2007, and the Great Wall of China is one of the winners.

新世界七大奇景的<u>結果</u>於2007年7月7日<u>公布</u>，中國的萬里長城為優勝者之一。
`98導遊`

▶ A <u>canal</u> <u>meanders</u> along a leafy bike pass, through green parks, and pass the city's four remaining windmills.

一條<u>運河</u>沿著葉子覆蓋著的單車道<u>蜿蜒而行</u>，穿過綠色公園和城市剩下4座的風車。 `101導遊`

▶ <u>Spectacular</u> fireworks shows lit up the sky of cities around the world as people <u>celebrated</u> the start of 2012.

<u>壯觀的</u>煙火照亮了世界上許多城市的天空，來<u>慶祝</u>2012年的開始。 `101導遊`

▶ The temple was really colorful. It had blue and red tiles all over it and there were <u>statues</u> of different gods on the walls and on the roof.

寺廟非常的色彩繽紛。鋪滿藍色和紅色的磁磚，且在牆上以及屋頂上有許多不同的神明<u>雕像</u>。 `100導遊`

▶ I'll pay a visit to the Wolfsonian, an extraordinary museum in Miami. I love its collection of decorative artifacts and propaganda materials from 1885 to 1945.

我會參觀沃爾夫索尼亞博物館，這間位於邁阿密的博物館很特別。我喜歡他的裝飾性藝術品以及1885年到1945年的宣傳資料收藏。 102導遊

▶ The landscape of this natural park is best seen on bike or foot, and there are numerous trails in the area. All paths offer breath-taking sceneries.

騎單車或是步行最能看出這個自然公園的景色，園內也有許多步道。所有小徑都能看到令人屏息的風景。 101導遊

▶ The view of cascading waterfalls in the rainforest is spectacular.

雨林中觀賞階梯狀的瀑布是很壯觀的。 101導遊

▶ People let off fireworks to celebrate New Year.

人們點燃煙火來慶祝新年。 99領隊

▶ Costa Brava is a popular tourist destination in northeastern Spain, thanks to its moderate climate, beautiful beaches, and charming towns.

西班牙東北部的布拉瓦海岸是很受歡迎的觀光景點，多虧了它溫和的氣候、美麗海灘和迷人小鎮。 101導遊

▶ My most memorable trip is climbing Mount Fuji. Getting to the peak and seeing the sunrise from the top of the clouds was amazing.

最令我念念不忘的旅行就是爬富士山。登頂在雲層上看日落真是太棒了。
101導遊

▶ A good place to end a tour of Rome is the Trevi Fountain. Legend has it that if you toss a single coin into the Trevi, you are guaranteed a return to Rome.

特雷維噴泉是結束羅馬之旅的好地方。傳説只要投一枚硬幣到噴泉內，就<u>保證</u>可以再訪羅馬。 `100導遊`

▶ Visitors to New York often talk about the feeling of <u>excitement</u> there. It is a city full of energy and hope.

拜訪紐約的遊客總是討論來此的<u>興奮</u>感。這是個充滿活力以及希望的城市。 `99導遊`

▶ Claire loves to buy <u>exotic</u> foods: vegetables and herbs from China, spices from India, olives from Greece, and cheeses from France.

克萊兒喜歡買<u>異國風情的</u>食物，來自中國的蔬菜和草藥、印度來的香料、希臘來的橄欖，以及法國來的起司。 `99導遊`

▶ Barcelona is beautiful but it's always <u>packed</u> with tourists in the summer.

巴塞隆納很漂亮，但夏天總是<u>塞滿</u>遊客。 `98導遊`

▶ The Louvre's Tactitle Gallery, specifically designed for <u>the blind and visually impaired</u>, is the only museum in France where visitors can touch the <u>sculptures</u>.

羅浮宮的觸感畫廊，專門替<u>盲人以及視障</u>所設計，這是法國唯一一個遊客可以觸摸<u>雕塑</u>的博物館。 `98導遊`

▶ Mount Fuji is considered <u>sacred</u>; therefore, many people <u>pay special visits</u> to it, wishing to bring good luck to themselves and their loved ones.

富士山被視為<u>神聖的</u>，因此許多人會<u>特別拜訪</u>，希望可以替自己以及所愛的人帶來好運。 `101領隊`

▶ Palm Beach is a coastline <u>resort</u> where thousands of tourists from all over the world spend their summer vacation.

棕櫚灘是海岸<u>度假勝地</u>，來自世界各地的上千名遊客都到此來度過暑假。 `101領隊`

torcar in the early 20th century. Railway companies in Europe and the United States used streamlined trains sin
high-speed services with an average speed of up to 130 km/h (80 mph) and a top speed of more than 160 km/h (1
e first high-speed train was the Italian ETR 200 that in July 1939 went from Milan to Florence at 165 km/h, wit
of 203 km/h. With this service, these trains were able to compete with the upcoming airplanes. In 1957, t
Electric Railway in Greater Tokyo launched its Romancecar 3000 SSE. This set a world record for narrow gau
45 km/h (90 mph), giving Japanese designers confidence that they could safely build even faster trains at standa
esperate for transport solutions due to overloaded trains between Tokyo and Osaka, the idea of high-speed rail w
apan. There is no globally accepted standard separating high-speed rail from conventional railroads; however
f widely accepted variables have been acknowledged by the industry in recent years. Generally, high-speed rai
s having a top speed in regular use of over 200 km/h (125 mph). A tour manager has individual duties to perform
r smoothly and successfully. For instance, the tour manager should always be the first one up every morning
nake sure each team member is ready before the bus leaves for the next scenic spot each day. The tour manager w

6. 飯店住宿

emergencies. Most importantly, the tour manager must take the group members home safe and sound at the end
ey and get ready for the next trip. Recently, a new type of tourism, or what is called 'alternative tourism', h
and become more and more popular among people who feel tired of the same old holidays and hope to gain real
experiences from traveling. This new kind of tourism takes the form of individual custom-made or independe
that take people to remote and exotic destinations, and cater to their different needs and interests. These holida
ally designed and arranged at a personal level. They often have different themes and offer a variety for people
om. As the market for this new form of tourism has expanded greatly, newer topics and programs will also app
s people begin to develop newer interests and needs in the future. But what exactly can people get out of alternati
For ecology-minded people, they can go whale-watching or take a conservation trip to help restore the damag
For people who like adventure and outdoor activities, the choices could range from mountain climbing, scu
indsurfing, white-water rafting to cycling in the mountains and deserts. For people who simply like to relax a
ace of mind, they can spend a week at spa and health resorts to relax and de-stress, or take yoga and meditati
country retreats in India. For people who are fond of culture and heritage, they can visit museums and art galler
York, take a weekend break at the Edinburgh International Festival, or tour around France to visit historic castl
ograms under alternative tourism include holidays that are taken for educational, artistic or religious purpos

提到於飯店下榻，除了價錢之外，設施以及服務則是一般人最大的考量。而到了旺季，訂房的順利與否也是很大的決定因素，因此與飯店住宿相關的實用單字，便是領隊導遊英文最重要的命題之一，在歷屆考題中幾乎都有出現，請務必熟讀！

130 km (80 mph) and a top speed of more than 160 km/h (100 mph). The first high-speed train was the Itali
that in July 1939 went from Milan to Florence at 165 km/h, with a top speed of 203 km/h. With this service, the
re able to compete with the upcoming airplanes. In 1957, the Odakyu Electric Railway in Greater Tokyo launch
ncecar 3000 SSE. This set a world record for narrow gauge trains at 145 km/h (90 mph), giving Japanese designe
ce that they could safely build even faster trains at standard gauge. Desperate for transport solutions due
d trains between Tokyo and Osaka, the idea of high-speed rail was born in Japan. There is no globally accept

關鍵單字

accommodation 住宿	boutique 流行女裝商店、精品店
lodging 住宿	file a complaint 投訴
bed down 下榻	alternative 其他的選擇
reserved （被）保留的	satisfactory 令人滿意的、符合要求的
reservation 預訂	unsatisfactory 不令人滿意的
vacant 空的	cater 迎合，或承辦伙食
vacancy 空房、空位	reception 接待處
room rate 房價	front desk 櫃台
in advance 事先	concierge 旅館服務台人員 / 門房
high season 旺季	hotel clerk 飯店人員
luxurious 奢華的	guest service 客戶服務
luxury 奢華	valet parking service 代客泊車
be ranked 被排名	concierge service 管家服務
be graded 被評分	feature 特色
be categorized 被分類	leave message 留話給……
delivery service 寄件服務	take message 幫……留話
panoramic 全景的	fill out registration form 填寫登記表格
complimentary 免費	airport limousine service 機場禮車接送服務
facility 設施	
amenities 設施	
parlor 休息室、接待室	

▶ If you plan and time it right, some <u>swapping</u> home can let you stay some-where for free.

如果你計劃且時機合適，有<u>些交換</u>住家可讓你免費入住。 101導遊

▶ A <u>reserved</u> room or seat is being kept for someone rather than given or sold to someone else.

<u>被保留的</u>房間或是座位是替某些人保留，不能提供或出售給他人。 100導遊

▶ You don't have to worry about where to stay tonight. My friend in <u>downtown area</u> will find you a <u>night's lodging</u>.

你不需去擔心今晚在哪過夜。我在<u>市區</u>的朋友會幫你找到<u>過夜的地方</u>。
99導遊

▶ It is the <u>high season</u>, and I'm not sure whether the hotel could provide enough <u>accommodations</u> for the whole group.

現在是<u>旺季</u>，我不確定飯店是否可以提供足夠的<u>住宿</u>給整個旅行團。 102領隊

▶ During the holidays, most major hotels will be <u>fully booked</u>. An <u>alternative</u> is to try and find a guest house near your desired destination.

假期期間，大部分主要的飯店都<u>被訂滿</u>了。<u>其他的選擇</u>只得試著找看看接近你目的地附近的民宿。 98導遊

▶ Jessica's customers complained because they had to pay twice for their <u>accommodation</u>.

潔西卡的客人有抱怨，因為他們必須支付兩次<u>住宿</u>費用。 100領隊

75

▶ Reservations for hotel accommodation should be made in advance to make sure rooms are available.

旅館的訂房應提早訂,才能確保有房間。 `98領隊`

▶ The hotels in the resort areas are fully booked in the summer. It would be very difficult to find any vacancies then.

度假勝地的飯店在夏天時被訂滿了。那時很難找到空房。 `102領隊`

▶ Either the reception or the cashier's desk of the hotel can help us figure out the exact amount of money and other details we need to join a local tour.

不是飯店的接待處就是收銀台,可以幫我們釐清正確的金額以及其他我們想參加當地旅遊的細節。 `102導遊`

▶ Tourists have a wide range of budget and tastes, and a wide variety of resorts and hotels have developed to cater for them.

觀光客有不同的預算以及品味,因此也有各式各樣的度假村和飯店來符合他們的需求。 `101導遊`

▶ Quick and friendly service at the front desk is important to the satisfaction of tourists.

櫃台的快速以及友善地服務對於觀光客的滿意度很重要。 `99導遊`

▶ Hotels are ranked internationally from one to five stars, depending on the services they offer and the prices of rooms.

國際上飯店被分級成一至五星級,是根據飯店所提供的服務以及房價所分類。
`98領隊`

▶ The "Ambassador" is centrally <u>located</u> in Hsinchu, a few minutes by car from the station. It offers a <u>panoramic</u> view of the metro Hsinchu area.

「國賓飯店」位於新竹的正中央，距離車站開車只要幾分鐘。它提供了新竹市區的全景。 102領隊

▶ Guest: I have made a reservation for a <u>suite</u> overnight.
　Clerk: Yes, we have your reservation right here. Would you please <u>fill out this registration form</u> and show me your ID?

客人：我已經訂了今晚的套房。
服務生：是的，我們這邊已經有您的訂房紀錄。麻煩您填上這個登記表格並出示您的證件。 102領隊

▶ A <u>complimentary</u> breakfast of coffee and rolls is served in the <u>lobby</u> between 7 and 10 am.

免費的早餐有咖啡和捲餅於早上7點到10點在大廳供應。 102領隊

▶ As for the <u>delivery service</u> of our hotel, FedEx and UPS can make <u>pickups</u> at the front desk Monday through Friday, <u>excluding</u> holidays.

關於我們飯店的寄件服務，聯邦快遞公司以及聯合包裹速遞公司會於週一至週五在櫃台取件，假日除外。 101領隊

▶ Working as a hotel <u>concierge</u> means that your focus is to <u>ensure</u> that the needs and requests of hotel guests are met, and that each guest has a memorable stay.

作為一位飯店的門房，表示你的重點是要確保客戶的需求與要求被滿足，讓每位房客有個難忘的停留回憶。 101領隊

▶ If you have to <u>extend</u> your stay at the hotel room, you should inform the front desk at least one day <u>prior to</u> your original departure time.

如果你必須<u>延長</u>在飯店房間的停留時間，你至少應該<u>在</u>原定離開時間<u>前</u>一天告知櫃台。 `101領隊`

▶ The hotel that he selected for the conference <u>featured</u> a nine-hole golf course.

他為這次記者會所選的旅館<u>以</u>九洞的高爾夫球場為<u>特色</u>。 `101領隊`

▶ Client: What are this hotel's <u>amenities</u>?
Agent: It includes a great restaurant, a fitness center, an outdoor pool, and much more, such as in-room Internet access, 24-hour room service, and <u>trustworthy</u> babysitting, etc.

客戶：這間飯店有什麼<u>設施</u>？
代理商：有一間很棒的餐廳、健身中心、戶外游泳池和其他設施，像是室內網路、24小時客房服務，和<u>值得信賴的</u>保母服務等。 `101領隊`

▶ Is there any problem with my <u>reservation</u>?

我的<u>預約</u>有任何問題嗎？ `100領隊`

▶ Guest: You have answered my questions <u>thoroughly</u>. Thank you very much.
Hotel clerk: You are welcome. <u>It's been my pleasure</u>.

客人：你很<u>詳細</u>地回答我的問題。非常謝謝你。
飯店人員：不客氣。<u>這是我的榮幸</u>。 `100領隊`

▶ This group of people would like to stay in <u>luxurious</u> hotels. They need to be five star hotels.

這群人想要住在<u>豪華</u>飯店。這些飯店必須要是五星級的。 `100領隊`

▶ The hotel services are far from <u>satisfactory</u>. I need to <u>file a complaint</u> with the manager.

飯店的服務完全稱不上<u>滿</u>意。我需要向經理<u>客訴</u>。 `99領隊`

▶ Guest: What <u>facilities</u> do you have in your hotel?

Hotel clerk: We have a fitness center, a swimming pool, two restaurants, a beauty parlor, and a boutique.

客人：你們飯店有什麼<u>設施</u>？

飯店人員：我們有健身中心、游泳池、兩間餐廳、美容室和精品店。 `99領隊`

▶ Guest: What is your <u>room rate</u>?

Hotel clerk: Our standard room costs NT$3,500 per night.

客人：你們的<u>房價</u>是多少？

飯店人員：我們的標準房每晚要價3,500元。 `99領隊`

▶ It's difficult to find a hotel with a/an <u>vacant</u> room in high season.

在旺季時很難找到有<u>空房</u>的飯店。 `99領隊`

▶ The caller: Can I speak to Ms. Taylor in room 612, please?

The operator: Please wait a minute. (pause) I'm sorry. There's no answer. May I <u>take</u> a message?

來電者：我可以和612號房的泰勒女士說話嗎？

接線生：請稍等。（停頓）我很抱歉。沒有人應答。我可以幫你<u>留話</u>嗎？
`99領隊`

▶ The <u>concierge</u> at the information desk in a hotel provides traveling information to guests.

<u>旅館服務台人員</u>提供旅遊資訊給客人。 `99領隊`

▶ The waiters will show you where to <u>bed down</u>.

服務生將告訴你會<u>下榻</u>在哪裡。 100領隊

▶ When you stay in a hotel, what basic <u>facilities</u> do you think are <u>necessary</u>?

當你住在飯店時，你認為哪些基本的<u>設備</u>是<u>必須的</u>？ 102領隊

▶ Airport limousine service, valet parking service, and concierge service are some of the most popular items among our <u>guest services</u>.

機場禮車接送服務、代客泊車、管家服務是我們最受歡迎的<u>客戶服務</u>項目之一。

102領隊

7. 餐廳 / 飲食

民以食為天，現代人除了重視日常生活的三餐之外，出外旅遊時品嚐美食也是一大重點，因此和吃有關，以及餐廳、點餐等相關英文，也不免俗地經常出現於考題中。

7. 餐廳 / 飲食

reserve 預約、預訂

make reservation 預約

reserve a table 訂桌

specialty 招牌菜

set meal 套餐

plate 盤子

bowl 碗

source 來源

authentic 道地的

sample 品嚐

delicacy 佳餚

stale 不新鮮的

fresh 新鮮的

staple 主食

catch on 流行起來

tolerance 容忍度

▶ If I had called to <u>reserve a table</u> at Royal House one week earlier, we would have had a gourmet reunion dinner last night.

如果我早一個星期打電話去皇家餐廳<u>訂桌</u>，我們昨晚可能就有美味的團圓飯。

`101領隊`

▶ This is a non-smoking restaurant. Please <u>put out</u> your cigarette at once.

這是禁菸餐廳。請立刻<u>熄滅</u>你的香菸。 `98領隊`

▶ Waiter: Are you ready to order, sir?

Guest: I think so. But what is your <u>specialty</u>?

服務生：你準備好要點餐了嗎，先生？

客人：應該是。但你們的<u>招牌菜</u>是什麼？ `99領隊`

▶ Our client wants to reserve a table for dinner tomorrow.

我們的客人想要為明天晚餐預先訂桌。 `100領隊`

▶ Would you like to order a/an set meal or refer to the à la carte menu?

你想要點套餐，還是參考菜單？ `100領隊`

▶ Sweets aren't an intrinsic part of a meal, but their presence on the dining table is often a great source of happiness.

甜點本來不是正餐中的一部分，但它在餐桌上的出現常成為快樂的來源。 `102領隊`

> ⚠ 重點：intrinsic 內部的、本體內的；source 來源。

▶ Three meals a day means that normally one will have breakfast, lunch and dinner each day.

一天三餐表示通常每天只會有早餐、午餐和晚餐。 `102領隊`

▶ This restaurant features authentic Northern Italian dishes that reflect the true flavors of Italy.

這間餐廳以反映義大利口味的道地北義大利菜為特色。 `101導遊`

▶ At the annual food festival, you can a sample wide variety of delicacies.

在一年一度的美食節，你可以品嚐各類佳餚。 `101領隊`

▶ Some people refuse to eat shark fin soup because it is made with parts of protected animals.

有些人拒絕食用魚翅湯，因為它是以受保護動物的某一部分所製成。 `100導遊`

▶ The cake was stale, and tasted bad.

這個蛋糕不新鮮了，且嚐起來不好吃。 `99導遊`

▶ Baked goods are not a staple of a traditional Chinese diet, but they have been quickly catching on among China's urban middle classes over the last 10 years.

烘培食品並非傳統中國菜的主菜，但過去10年，這些已經在中國城市的中產階級之間快速地流行。 100導遊

▶ People with a low tolerance for spicy food should not try the "Hot and Spicy Chicken Soup" served by this restaurant: it brings tears to my eyes.

對於辛辣食物容忍度低的人不應該試此餐廳的「麻辣雞湯」，它讓我眼淚直流。 99導遊

▶ Many restaurants in Paris offer a plate of snails for guests to taste.

巴黎的許多餐廳提供一整盤的蝸牛給顧客吃。 99領隊

▶ Slices of lamb are grilled or fried in butter and served with mushrooms, onions, and chips.

一片片的烤羊肉或是用奶油炸的羊肉，佐上蘑菇、洋蔥和薯片。 99領隊

⚠ 重點：grill 烤，通常熱源只有單面，像是中秋烤肉。

8. 社交禮儀

　　不論是出國帶團（領隊），或是向外國人介紹台灣（導遊），都會和不同文化的人交流，因此適當的社交禮儀便成為非常重要的課題。然而以此社交禮儀的文化命題下，以華人社會來說，婚姻乃是人生大事，因此看似和旅遊無關聯的考題分類，卻也經常出現於考題中。

禮儀準則

greet 問候

greetings 問候語

custom 風俗

customary 約定俗成的

customs 海關

social manner 社交禮儀

dress code 穿衣法則

occasion 場合

personnel 人員

personality 外在的性格

character 內在的特質

table manner 餐桌禮儀

dos and don'ts 可做與不可做的
（注意事項）

appropriate / inappropriate
合宜的 / 不合宜的

polite / impolite 禮貌的 / 不禮貌的

When in Rome, do as the Romans
do. 入境隨俗。

▶ When Latin Americans and Middle Easterners <u>greet</u> each other, they tend to stand closer together when talking than Americans do.

當拉丁美洲人和中東人彼此<u>打招呼</u>時，他們傾向站得比美國人交談時更近。
`98導遊`

▶ In most western countries, it's <u>customary</u> for you to bring a bottle of wine or a box of candy as a gift when you are invited for dinner at someone's home.

在大多數的西方國家中，當你去其他人家作客時，帶一瓶紅酒或是一箱糖果當作伴手禮是種<u>基本禮儀（約定俗成的事）</u>。 `98導遊`

▶ Dress codes are basically some dos and don'ts about what people wear in an organization or on a particular occasion.

穿衣法則基本上有些行為準則，關於人們在哪個組織或是特殊場合應該穿什麼樣的衣服。 102導遊

▶ If we remember our social manners, particularly in a big crowd, we shall win people's admiration though we may not feel it.

如果我們記得我們的社交禮儀，特別是在群眾中，即便我們沒有感覺到，我們應該會贏得人們的尊敬。 102導遊

▶ When Americans shake hands, they do so firmly, not loosely. In the American culture, a weak handshake is a sign of weak character.

當美國人握手時，會握得較為強而有力，而不是無力的。在美國人的文化中，蜻蜓點水的握手方式則為軟弱特質的象徵。 98導遊

▶ In many Western cultures, it is rude to ask about a person's age, weight, or salary. However, these topics may not be as sensitive in East Asia.

在許多西方國家，問他人的年齡、體重，或是薪水是很無禮的。然而這些話題在東亞可能就不是如此敏感。 99導遊

▶ Table manners differ from culture to culture. In Italy, it is considered inappropriate for a woman to pour her neighbor a glass of wine.

每個文化的餐桌禮儀都不同。在義大利，女士幫鄰座倒酒就被視為不恰當的行為。 98導遊

▶ Do not be afraid to eat with your hands here. When in Rome, do as the Romans do.

在這裡不要害怕用手吃飯。要入境隨俗。 100領隊

婚姻大事

newlywed 新婚夫婦

bachelor 單身漢

tie the knot 結婚

groom 新郎

bride 新娘

bridal tour、honeymoon 蜜月旅行

wedding anniversary 結婚周年

divorce 離婚

file for divorce 提出離婚訴訟

have an affair with 與……有染

available 可獲得的

significant 有意義的、重要的

phenomenon 現象

▶ Because son preference has been a significant <u>phenomenon</u> in Asia for centuries, the Chinese actually have a term for such <u>bachelors</u>: "bare branches" – branches of the family tree that will never bear fruit.

幾個世紀以來，由於重男輕女在亞洲都是很重要的<u>現象</u>，中國甚至稱<u>單身漢</u>為「光棍」——光棍不能為家庭開花結果。 100導遊

▶ The <u>wedding anniversary</u> is worth celebrating.

<u>結婚周年</u>很值得慶祝。 100領隊

> ⚠ 重點：「worth of + 動名詞」與「worth + 動名詞」兩者形式不同，但意思相同。
> worth of + 動名詞是「被動式的動名詞」；而worth後面接主動式的動名詞，雖然在形式上是主動的，但其意義仍然是被動的。如 The wedding anniversary is worth of being celebrating. = The wedding anniversary is worth celebrating.

▶ It is said that there are only a few lucky days <u>available</u> for getting married in 2010.

據說2010年只有幾天好日子<u>可以</u>結婚。 `99領隊`

▶ Mary is <u>filing for divorce</u> because her husband is <u>having an affair with</u> his secretary.

瑪莉<u>提出離婚訴訟</u>，因為她的丈夫與其祕書<u>有染</u>。 `99領隊`

> ⚠ 重點：file除了當名詞「檔案」外，當動詞有提出的意思。例句：The hotel services are far from satisfactory. I need to file a complaint with the manager. 飯店的服務讓人無法滿意。我需要向經理客訴。 `99領隊`

▶ The newlyweds are on their <u>bridal tour</u>.

新婚夫婦正在<u>蜜月旅行</u>。 `100領隊`

> ⚠ 重點：newlyweds 新婚夫婦；bridal tour = honeymoon 蜜月旅行。

▶ While many couples opt for a church wedding and wedding party, a Japanese groom and a Taiwanese bride <u>tied the knot</u> in a traditional Confucian wedding in Taipei.

當許多情侶選擇教堂婚禮以及婚宴時，一對日本新郎以及台灣新娘在台北選擇傳統的儒家婚禮<u>互訂終身</u>。 `101領隊`

9. 領隊導遊職責

領隊、導遊實際上帶團的作業項目，也經常出現於考題中。這些不外乎是工作上的挑戰、與旅行社的配合（訂房事宜），或是交通工具的安排、景點介紹等等。這部分除了筆試之外，也是英語導遊口試時可能出現的考題。這部分所列的嚴選佳句相對簡單，建議一句句大聲唸出來，亦可練習語感。

關鍵單字

tour guide 導遊	manner 態度、禮貌
tour manager 領隊	sunny 陽光性格的
travel agent 旅行社	outgoing 外向的
Tourism Bureau 觀光旅遊局	shy 害羞的
in peak season 旺季	humble、modest 謙虛的
committed 致力於	first impression 第一印象
responsible for 對……有責任	sit back 放鬆休息
challenge 挑戰	courteous、well-mannered、polite 禮貌的
mingle 使混合、使相混	discourteous、ill-mannered、impolite 沒禮貌的
shuttle bus 接駁車	seniors 長者，也可當作前輩、資深人士
deposit 訂金	rely on、depend on、count on 依靠、信賴
make reservation 訂位	
secure reservation 確保訂位 / 房	
re-confirmation 再確認	
broaden horizons 開拓視野	

嚴選佳句

▶ A good <u>tour guide</u> has to be <u>committed</u> to the people in his group.

一名好的導遊必須致力於照顧他的團員。 101導遊

▶ A <u>tour guide</u> is <u>responsible for</u> informing tourists about the culture and the beautiful sites of a city or town.

導遊應負責告知遊客該城鎮的文化和美麗的景點。 101領隊

▶ As a <u>tour guide</u>, you will face new <u>challenges</u> every day. One of the hardest parts of your job may be answering questions.

身為<u>導遊</u>，每天會面臨到新的<u>挑戰</u>。最困難的工作之一也許就是回答問題。
98導遊

▶ Mingling with tourists from different backgrounds helps tour guides <u>broaden their horizons</u> and learn new things in answering curious visitors' various questions.

與不同背景的觀光客打交道幫助導遊<u>開拓視野</u>，也學習回答好奇的旅客不同的新問題。 102導遊

▶ The tour guide is a <u>courteous</u> man; he is very polite and always speaks in a kind manner.

導遊是一個<u>有教養的</u>男生，他非常禮貌，談吐也得宜。 101導遊

▶ The local tour guide has a <u>sunny</u> personality. Everybody likes him.

這位當地的導遊有著<u>陽光開朗的</u>性格。每個人都喜歡他。 101導遊

▶ Before we left the hotel, our tour guide gave us a thirty-minute <u>presentation</u> on the local culture.

在我們離開旅館之前，我們的導遊做了30分鐘當地文化的<u>簡報介紹</u>。 101導遊

▶ Being a tour guide is a very important job. In many cases, the tour guide is the traveler's first <u>impression</u> of our country.

當一個導遊是一份很重要的工作。在許多情形下，導遊是遊客對我們國家的第一<u>印象</u>。 98導遊

▶ Mr. Jones has <u>got the hang</u> of being a tour guide.

Mr. Jones has <u>learned the skills</u> of being a tour guide.

瓊斯先生已經<u>學習</u>到當一位導遊的<u>技巧</u>。 `100領隊`

▶ The tour guide <u>persuaded</u> him into buying some expensive <u>souvenirs</u>.

這名導遊<u>說服</u>他買昂貴的<u>紀念品</u>。 `100領隊`

▶ We were asked by our tour guide on the <u>shuttle bus</u> to <u>remain</u> seated until we <u>reached</u> our destination.

導遊要求我們<u>待</u>在<u>接駁車</u>的座位上，直到<u>抵達</u>目的地。 `98導遊`

▶ We're going to be driving through farmland for the next twenty minutes or so, so just <u>sit back</u> and relax until we're closer to the city.

接下來大約20分鐘的車程我們會駛經農田，所以在接近市區之前，請輕鬆<u>就坐</u>。 `98導遊`

▶ If you want to become a successful <u>tour manager</u>, you have to work <u>hard</u> and learn from <u>the seniors</u>.

如果你想成為一名成功的<u>領隊</u>，你必須<u>很努力地</u>工作並向<u>前輩</u>學習。 `98領隊`

▶ In order to make traveling easier, especially for those who <u>rely on</u> public transportation, the <u>Tourism Bureau</u> worked with local governments to <u>initiate</u> the Taiwan Tourist Shuttle Service in 2010.

為了讓旅遊更容易，特別是針對那些仰賴大眾運輸的人，<u>觀光旅遊局</u>與當地政府一起於2010年<u>開始實施</u>台灣旅遊巴士服務。 `102導遊`

▶ In case you need to <u>get in touch with me</u>, you can reach me at 224338654 at my <u>travel agency</u>.

萬一你需要<u>和我聯繫</u>，你可以打224338654到我的<u>旅行社</u>和我聯絡。 `100導遊`

▶ For tours in peak seasons, travel agents sometimes have to make reservations a year or more in advance.

對於旺季的出遊，旅行社有時必須早在一年之前、甚至更早就事先預定好行程。 99導遊

▶ The travel agent says that we have to pay a deposit of $2,000 in advance in order to secure the reservation for our hotel room.

旅行社說我們必須事先支付2,000元訂金，來確保飯店訂房。 98導遊

▶ The travel agent apologized for the delay.

旅行社因為行程延誤而道歉。 100領隊

motorcar in the early 20th century. Railway companies in Europe and the United States used streamlined tra
933 for high-speed services with an average speed of up to 130 km/h (80 mph) and a top speed of more than
100 mph). The first high-speed train was the Italian ETR 200 that in July 1939 went from Milan to Florence at
with a top speed of 203 km/h. With this service, these trains were able to compete with the upcoming airplanes
the Odakyu Electric Railway in Greater Tokyo launched its Romancecar 3000 SSE. This set a world record
gauge trains at 145 km/h (90 mph), giving Japanese designers confidence that they could safely build even fas
at standard gauge. Desperate for transport solutions due to overloaded trains between Tokyo and Osaka, the idea
eed rail was born in Japan. There is no globally accepted standard separating high-speed rail from conventio
ds; however, a number of widely accepted variables have been acknowledged by the industry in recent yea
ly, high-speed rail is defined as having a top speed in regular use of over 200 km/h (125 mph). A tour manager
ual duties to perform to run a tour smoothly and successfully. For instance, the tour manager should always be
e up every morning in order to make sure each team member is ready before the bus leaves for the next scenic s

10. 國家大事

ns, such as stolen passports, physical ailments and medical emergencies. Most importantly, the tour manager m
e group members home safe and sound at the end of the journey and get ready for the next trip. Recently, a n
tourism, or what is called 'alternative tourism', has emerged and become more and more popular among peo
el tired of the same old holidays and hope to gain real or authentic experiences from traveling. This new kind
n takes the form of individual custom-made or independent holidays that take people to remote and exo
tions, and cater to their different needs and interests. These holidays are basically designed and arranged a
l level. They often have different themes and offer a variety for people to choose from. As the market for this n
f tourism has expanded greatly, newer topics and programs will also appear as long as people begin to deve
interests and needs in the future. But what exactly can people get out of alternative tourism? For ecology-min
they can go whale-watching or take a conservation trip to help restore the damaged coastline. For people who li
ure and outdoor activities, the choices could range from mountain climbing, scuba diving, windsurfing, white-wa
to cycling in the mountains and deserts. For people who simply like to relax and gain a peace of mind, they c
a week at spa and health resorts to relax and de-stress, or take yoga and meditation lessons at country retreats
For people who are fond of culture and heritage, they can visit museums and art galleries in New York, take
d break at the Edinburgh International Festival, or tour around France to visit historic castles. Other progra
alternative tourism include holidays that are taken for educational, artistic or religious purposes. These conta
English on a four-week trip to Australia, learning musical skills in the involved learning how to paint or hand
uring a   ent kinds
ns are   ce of n
s sign   ng faces
n, but   rm of ma
rtation   e early 20
. Railw   eed servic

國家的政策、法律等政治相關嚴肅議題，也會因時事而不時成
為考題，像是全球化的移民問題等等。乍看之下似乎考題偏難，其
實只要掌握重點單字，即可跨越障礙，輕鬆解題。

average speed of up to 130 km/h (80 mph) and a top speed of more than 160 km/h (100 mph). The first high-spe
as the Italian ETR 200 that in July 1939 went from Milan to Florence at 165 km/h, with a top speed of 203 km
is service, these trains were able to compete with the upcoming airplanes. In 1957, the Odakyu Electric Railway
Tokyo launched its Romancecar 3000 SSE. This set a world record for narrow gauge trains at 145 km/h (90 mp
Japanese designers confidence that they could safely build even faster trains at standard gauge. Desperate f

關鍵單字

legalize 合法化	census 人口普查
approval 同意	metropolitan / urban area 都會區
bill 法案	rural areas 鄉村、郊區
momentum 勢力	telephone fraud 電話詐欺
congress 立法機關	fraud 欺騙（行為）、詭計、騙局
custody 監護權	eliminate 消滅
court 法院	welfare 福利的一種
agreement 協議	income 收入、所得
immigration 移民	precaution 預防
immigrant 移民者	caution 警告
imminent 逼近的、即將發生的	urge 催促、力勸
financial crisis 金融危機	outbreak 暴動
impose 徵（稅）	indifference 漠不關心
cripple 嚴重毀壞或損害	difference 不同之處
cross-strait relations 兩岸關係	democratic 民主的

嚴選佳句

▶ A bill to <u>legalize</u> gay marriage in Washington State has won final legislative <u>approval</u> and taken effect starting 2012.

華盛頓州同性婚姻合法化的法案已經通過了最後立法同意，並於2012年生效。

`102導遊`

▶ The support for <u>suspending death penalty</u> has gained <u>momentum</u>, and it is very likely that someday the congress of the country will pass its suspension.

支持<u>廢死</u>已越來越有<u>勢力</u>，很有可能某天國會會通過廢死。 102導遊

▶ While <u>courts</u> in the U.S. generally <u>favor</u> the mother in the event of a divorce, Taiwan family and divorce laws will grant <u>custody</u> to the father, unless some other <u>agreement</u> is reached.

美國<u>法院</u>通常於夫妻離婚時會偏向女方，但台灣的親屬法則是偏判給父親<u>監護</u><u>權</u>，除非事先有達成<u>協議</u>。 100導遊

▶ Despite facing an <u>imminent labor shortage</u> as its population ages, Japan has done little to open itself up to <u>immigration</u>.

即便隨著人口高齡化，<u>勞工短缺</u>的問題近在眼前，日本開放<u>移民</u>方面還是做得很少。 100導遊

▶ According to a new study, the continuing arrival of <u>immigrants</u> to American shores is encouraging business activity and producing more jobs with the supply of abundant labors.

根據新的研究，美國海岸持續到來的<u>移民者</u>會讓商業發展更佳，也會產生更多的工作機會。 102導遊

▶ The <u>financial crisis</u> that started in the U.S. and swept the globe was further proof that—for better and for worse—we can't escape one another.

<u>金融危機</u>始於美國，且橫掃全球，更佳證明了——不管是好是壞，我們誰都逃不過。 102導遊

▶ Taiwan government said yesterday it will not give up <u>restrictions it imposes</u> <u>on imported beef</u>, after a warning by U.S. lawmakers that the issue could <u>cripple</u> free trade talks.

台灣政府昨天表示不會放棄對於進口牛肉課稅的限制，在經過美國立法單位警告之後，這項議題會破壞自由貿易。 102導遊

▶ Taiwan's premier said 2010 was a boom year for tourism in Taiwan and he attributed the success to the improvements in cross-strait relations.

台灣的行政院長說2010年是台灣旅遊業大幅成長的一年，他將此成功歸因於兩岸關係的改善。 100導遊

▶ Most countries take a census every ten years or so in order to count the people and to know where they are living.

大部分的國家每10年做一次人口普查，以計算人口以及其居住地。 100導遊

▶ The Taiwan High Prosecutors Office vowed to harshly crack down on anyone caught hoarding food staples as part of the government's efforts to stabilize food prices amid a string of price hikes following the Lunar New Year.

隨著農曆新年的到來，台灣高等法院檢察署嚴厲地打擊任何囤積大宗食物的行為，並依此作為政府穩定物價上漲的一連串措施。 100導遊

▶ The Ministry of the Interior has decided to eliminate telephone fraud.

內政部長決定消滅電話詐騙。 99領隊

▶ People who earn little or no income can receive public assistance, often called welfare.

賺很少或沒賺錢的人可以有大眾救助，常常稱為福利。 100導遊

▶ The Department of Health urged the public to receive H1N1 flu shot as a precaution against potential outbreaks.

衛生處勸導大眾接受H1N1流感疫苗作為預防，以對抗潛在的爆發。 99領隊

▶ Public <u>indifference</u> to voting is a problem in many <u>democratic</u> countries with low turnouts in elections.

大眾對於投票的<u>漠不關心</u>且投票率低是許多<u>民主</u>國家的問題。 98領隊

▶ Martial law was <u>lifted</u> from Matsu in 1992, a number of years later than "mainland" Taiwan. Matsu residents are now allowed to travel freely to and from Taiwan.

馬祖在1992年<u>解除戒嚴</u>，比起台灣本島慢了幾年。現在馬祖居民可以自由往返台灣。 100導遊

⚠ 重點：此處考lift，除了舉起，還有取消之意。

11. 社會現象

與國家大事不同，此分類著重於目前世界的走向、趨勢，以及目前台灣社會的概況。而由於網路的興起所造成的各類社會現象，也是近年來熱門的考題。

cellphone、mobile phone 手機

heavy user 重度使用者

flourish 蓬勃發展

smother 阻擋、阻礙

handy 方便

poverty 貧窮、貧困

lift oneself out of poverty 讓某人脫貧

fosters equality 促進平等

social isolation 社會隔離

population 人口

ethics 道德

within the law 合法

compulsory 義務的

environmentally friendly 對生態環境無害的

outdated、obsolete 過時的

old-fashioned 舊式的

modern 現代的

notion 概念、想法

take place 舉行、發生

replace 取代

metropolitan 大都市的

urban 都會的

rural 鄉村的

demographers 人口統計學家

decline 下降、減少

national treasure 國家寶藏，也作「台灣之光」

▶ Simply put, no society can truly <u>flourish</u> if it <u>smothers</u> the dreams and productivity of half its population, women.

簡單來説，如果它<u>阻擋</u>了一半的人口──女性的夢想以及生產力，沒有一個社會可以真正地<u>蓬勃發展</u>。 102導遊

▶ The cellphone is very <u>handy</u> because it connects us with the world at large and even <u>provides</u> us with the necessary information on crucial moments.

手機非常的<u>方便</u>，因為它讓我們充分和世界溝通，甚至在重要時刻<u>提供</u>我們所需的資訊。 `102導遊`

▶ Technology, such as cellphones, often <u>fosters</u> equality and helps lift people <u>out of poverty</u>.

科技，像是手機，常常<u>促進</u>平等並且幫助人們<u>脫貧</u>。 `102導遊`

▶ Many users of mobile phones would get <u>heavy</u> anxious and panic once the phone is missing.

一旦手機不見時，許多手機的使用者都會<u>重度</u>焦慮或慌張。 `102領隊`

▶ The Internet is creating <u>social isolation</u> as people are spending more time on computers.

網路正造成<u>社會隔離</u>，因為人們花更多的時間在電腦上。 `101領隊`

▶ Seeing the <u>rise</u> of new media technology, many people predict newspapers will soon be <u>obsolete</u>.

看見了新媒體科技的<u>崛起</u>，很多人預測報紙很快就會<u>過時</u>。 `102領隊`
※rise用法詳見P.51。

▶ The notion that fashionable shopping takes place only in cities is <u>outdated</u>, thanks to the Internet.

歸功於網路，去大城市購物才時髦這樣的觀念已經<u>過時</u>了。 `101導遊`

▶ The <u>Industrial Revolution</u>, which began in the nineteenth century, caused <u>widespread</u> unemployment as machines replaced workers.

<u>工業革命</u>，始於19世紀，由於機器取代勞工，導致<u>普遍的失業</u>。 `100導遊`

▶ <u>Metropolitan</u> areas are more densely populated than <u>rural areas</u>. That is, they have more people per square mile.

大都會區的人口密度比鄉村來得高。也就是每平方英里有比較多的人。 〔100導遊〕

▶ <u>Demographers</u> study population growth or decline and things like <u>urbanization</u>, which means the movement of <u>populations</u> into cities.

人口統計學家研究人口的成長或是削減,像是都市化表示<u>人口</u>往城市移動。
〔100導遊〕

▶ In 2060, people over 65 will account for more than 41 percent of the <u>population</u> in Taiwan.

2060年,65歲以上的人口將會超過台灣<u>人口</u>總數的41%。 〔102領隊〕

> ⚠ 重點:account for有「說明(原因、理由等)」、「導致、引起」、「(在數量、比例上)占」、「對……負責」之意。例句:How do you account for the company's alarmingly high staff turnover? 你怎麼解釋這家公司高得令人憂心的人員流動率?

▶ Many couples live together even though they are not married. The <u>ethics</u> of their behavior are <u>highly suspect</u>, but technically they are <u>within the law</u>.

許多情侶在還沒結婚前同居。他們的<u>道德</u>行為被<u>高度質疑</u>,但技術上來說他們是<u>合法的</u>。 〔100導遊〕

▶ As introductory English now begins in elementary, rather than secondary school, and classes have begun to focus more on the <u>spoken language</u>, travelers to Taiwan can <u>get by</u> without having to attempt any Mandarin or Taiwanese.

英語入門始於小學而非國中,且課程也著重在<u>口語</u>,到台灣的旅客可以<u>勉強</u>用英文溝通,而不用講中文或是台語。 〔100導遊〕

▶ The public education in Taiwan has been <u>compulsory</u> from primary school through junior high school since 1968.

台灣的大眾教育自從1968年來，從小學到國中都是<u>義務</u>教育。 `100導遊`

▶ Living in a highly <u>competitive</u> society, some Taiwanese children are forced by their parents to learn many <u>skills</u> at a very young age.

生活在高度<u>競爭</u>的社會，有些台灣小孩從小就被逼著學很多<u>技能</u>。 `99領隊`

▶ Violent video games have been <u>blamed for</u> school shootings, increases in <u>bullying</u>, and violence towards women.

暴力的遊戲被<u>歸咎</u>於導致校園槍械，增加<u>霸凌</u>，以及對於女性的暴力。 `102領隊`

▶ More and more Taiwanese have come to view <u>cycling</u> not only as a form of <u>recreation</u> but as a way of being environmentally <u>friendly</u>.

越來越多台灣人不只將<u>單車</u>視為一項<u>休閒活動</u>，也是<u>友善</u>環境的一項作法。 `98導遊`

> ⚠ 重點：environmentally friendly 對生態環境無害的，常見的還有user friendly 易使用的，通常用來形容軟硬體的操作介面。

❀ The <u>birth rate</u> in Taiwan was at a/an <u>record</u> low last year.

台灣的<u>出生率</u>和去年比起來達到<u>紀錄</u>低點。 `99領隊`

▶ Baseball is the number one team sport here in Taiwan. The most accomplished player, New York Yankees' Wang Chien-ming, is <u>frequently</u> referred to as a <u>national treasure</u>.

棒球在台灣是第一名的團體運動，最有成就的球員——紐約洋基的王建民，<u>常常被稱為台灣之光</u>。 `98導遊`

12. 介紹台灣

關於台灣的點點滴滴，考題總是五花八門。此處與其它分類不同，會有許多共同單字，因此一併整理成一單字列表。此分類除了筆試外，也常出現於口試中，故其重要性不言而喻。

spectacle 奇觀

marvelous scenery 絕美風光

urban 城市的

rustic 鄉下的

rural 農村的、田園的

export 出口

import 進口

retreat 僻靜之處

ecology 生態環境

spring 溫泉

take in 欣賞、參觀

indigenous 本地的、土生土長的

serene 寧靜的

peak 山峰、高峰

Mandarin 中文

demonstrate 論證、證明

a must-see for visitors 必遊景點

calligraphy 書法

derive from 衍生出

perform 表演

National Palace Museum 故宮博物院

collection 收藏品

rural folk culture 民俗文化

fireworks 煙火

firecrackers 鞭炮

symbol 符號

symbolize 象徵

custom 風俗

customs 海關

customary 約定俗成的

souvenir 紀念品

indigenous 土生土長的

local snack 當地小吃

authentic 道地的

throng 人群

highlight 亮點

fascinate 迷住、強烈地吸引

tourist destinations、tourist spots、tourist attractions 觀光景點

scenic spots 風景景點

well known、famous、renowned 有名的

second to none 不亞於任何人、首屈一指

城市風情

▶ Bopiliao, <u>located</u> in Wanhua District, Taipei, and serving as the setting for the film, Monga, is a popular <u>tourist spot</u>.

剝皮寮<u>位於</u>台北萬華區，曾是電影《艋舺》拍片的場景，是個受歡迎的<u>觀光景點</u>。 `101導遊`

▶ Chichi is a town in Central Taiwan that is <u>accessible</u> by rail.

集集是中台灣鐵路<u>可到達</u>的城鎮。 `101導遊`

> ⚠ 重點：形容某處的交通時，經常用accessible by car / rail來形容（是否能開車、搭火車到達）。

▶ One of Hualien's long-standing traditions is <u>stone carving</u>, which is not surprising considering the city's main <u>export</u> is marble.

花蓮屹立不搖的傳統之一就是<u>石雕</u>，因此此城市的主要<u>出口</u>為大理石也就不足為奇了。 `100導遊`

▶ Pingxi District in New Taipei City of Taiwan <u>holds an annual Lantern Festival</u> in which <u>releasing sky lanterns</u> has become a tradition. <u>Legend has it</u> that sky lanterns were the invention of an ancient Chinese politician and military leader "Kong Ming."

台灣新北市的平溪區<u>舉辦</u>一年一度的燈籠節，<u>放天燈</u>已經變成是一種傳統。<u>據說</u>天燈是古代中國政治家，也是軍事領導者「孔明」的發明。 `102導遊`

自然風景

▶ Wulai is a famous hot-spring <u>resort</u>.

烏來是著名的溫泉<u>度假勝地</u>。 100領隊

▶ Taroko National Park <u>features</u> high mountains and <u>steep canyons</u>. Many of its peaks tower above 3,000 meters in elevation.

太魯閣國家公園<u>以</u>高山以及<u>陡峭的峽谷為</u>特色。許多高峰海拔超過3,000公尺。
101導遊

▶ Many tourists are <u>fascinated</u> by the natural <u>spectacles</u> of Taroko Gorge.

許多觀光客為太魯閣的<u>自然奇觀</u>所著迷。 98領隊

▶ Many people consider Yangmingshan National Park a pleasant <u>retreat</u> from the bustle of the city.

許多人認為陽明山國家公園是個遠離城市喧囂的<u>僻靜之處</u>。 100導遊

▶ Besides <u>participating in</u> local cultural activities, people who desire to explore the <u>ecology</u> of Kenting can observe plenty of wildlife and plants.

除了<u>參與</u>當地文化活動外，想在墾丁探訪<u>生態環境</u>的人也可以觀察豐富的野生動物與植物。 99導遊

▶ Unlike other springs locations, Taian Hot Springs is relatively <u>serene</u>, with no more than six large-scale resorts in the area, so the place is not as <u>congested</u> as Wulai and Beitou.

不像其他溫泉地區，泰安溫泉相對<u>安靜</u>，這區域的大型渡假村不超過6個，所以不像烏來和北投一樣<u>擁擠</u>。 100導遊

▶ Wind and sunshine are very important <u>assets</u> for Penghu, attracting a large number of tourists each year.

風和陽光是澎湖很重要的<u>資產</u>，每年吸引了大批觀光客到來。 99導遊

▶ With crystal clear water, emerald green mountains and various outdoor activities to offer, it's not <u>surprising</u> that Sun Moon Lake is one of <u>the most visited spots</u> in Taiwan.

有著清澈的水、翠綠的山脈，以及多種戶外活動可選，日月潭是台灣<u>遊客最多</u>的景點之一並<u>不讓人驚訝</u>。 101導遊

▶ Taiwan is well known for its mountain <u>scenic spots</u> and <u>urban landmarks</u> such as the National Palace Museum and the Taipei 101 skyscraper.

台灣以其高山<u>風景景點</u>，以及<u>城市的地標</u>，像是故宮博物院和台北101摩天大樓聞名。 101導遊

▶ Ku-Kuan, east of Tai-Chung City, with its <u>steep cliffs</u>, has become a <u>paradise</u> for rock climbers here in Taiwan.

谷關，位於台中市東部，有著陡峭的懸崖，已經成為台灣登山者的<u>天堂</u>。 98導遊

> ⚠ 重點：paradise 天堂，亦常用heaven替代。兩者雖在口語上經常相互使用，但paradise這個字其實是人間仙境的意思；而heaven則是另一個世界的天堂。

▶ When visiting Alishan, one of the most popular tourist destinations in Taiwan, it's worth spending a few days to learn about the indigenous people living in mountain villages and <u>take in</u> the <u>marvelous scenery</u>.

當去最受歡迎的台灣觀光景點——阿里山旅遊時，很值得花幾天去學習原住民的高山生活方式，和<u>欣賞 絕美風光</u>。 102導遊

▶ At 3,952 meters, Yushan is not only Taiwan's tallest <u>peak</u>; it is also the tallest mountain in Northeast Asia.

高3,952公尺，玉山不只是台灣的最高峰，也是東北亞的最高峰。 102導遊

▶ Taiwan has plentiful annual <u>rainfall</u> but unfortunately its rivers are too short and too close to the sea.

台灣有很豐沛的降雨，但很不幸的河流太短且太靠近海。 102導遊

藝術文化

▶ With 49 shops around the island, Eslite Bookstore was <u>selected</u> by Time magazine in 2004 as <u>a must-see for visitors</u> to Taiwan.

在台灣島上有49間營業據點，誠品書店於2004年被時代雜誌<u>選為</u>台灣的<u>必遊景點</u>。 98導遊

▶ Opened in May 2008, the Children's Gallery of the <u>National Palace Museum</u> is <u>aimed at</u> children between the ages of 7 and 12.

2008年5月開幕，<u>故宮博物院</u>的兒童畫廊是以7-12歲的兒童為<u>對象</u>。 98導遊

▶ There are around 7,000 convenience stores in Taiwan, the highest concentration in the world. The <u>ubiquitous</u> 7-Eleven chain offers a great range of services, from faxing and copying to bill payments for customers.

台灣大約有7,000間便利商店，是全世界密度最高的。<u>到處都有的</u>7-11連鎖店則是提供顧客各<u>類型</u>的服務，從傳真、影印到付款。 100導遊

▶ Cloud Gate, an internationally <u>renowned</u> dance group from Taiwan, <u>demonstrated</u> that the quality of modern dance in Asia could be <u>comparable</u> to that of modern dance in Europe and North America.

雲門，來自台灣的國際<u>知名</u>舞蹈團體，<u>證明</u>亞洲現代舞水準可和歐洲以及北美的現代舞<u>媲美</u>。 101導遊

▶ Cursive II is a recent work of Taiwan's master choreographer Lin Hwai-min. He created Cursive, with its title <u>derived</u> from Chinese <u>calligraphy</u>.

《行草貳》是台灣編舞家林懷民最近的作品。他創造的行草名稱<u>來源</u>則是來自中國<u>書法</u>。 100導遊

▶ Formed in 1991 and having <u>toured</u> internationally in Europe and Asia, the Formosa Aboriginal Dance Troupe is a group that <u>performs</u> Taiwanese folk music.

成立於1991年，也曾於歐洲以及亞洲<u>巡迴</u>過，福爾摩沙原住民舞蹈團<u>演奏</u>台灣民俗音樂。 98導遊

▶ For a lot of foreigners, the hardest thing about learning <u>Mandarin</u> is its tones. If you use the wrong one, you <u>end up</u> saying the wrong word.

對大多數的外國人來說，學習<u>中文</u>最難的就是音調。如果你的音調發錯，<u>最後</u>發出來的字也是錯的。 98導遊

▶ Taiwan has more than 400 museums. The most famous of these is the <u>National Palace Museum</u>, which holds the world's largest <u>collection</u> of Chinese art treasures.

台灣有400間以上的博物館。其中最有名的為<u>故宮博物院</u>，它擁有世界上最多的中華文物<u>收藏品</u>。 98導遊

> ⚠ 重點：hold除了手握，亦可為舉辦，此處則為擁有。用法詳見P.120。

▶ The National Palace Museum opens daily from 9 a.m. to 5 p.m.. However, for Saturdays, the hours are <u>extended</u> to 8:30 p.m..

故宮博物院每天從早上9點開放至下午5點。但每個星期六開放時間則<u>延長</u>到晚上8點半。 98導遊

▶ The Presidential Office in Taiwan is a classic <u>mix</u> of European renaissance and baroque style architecture, <u>combining</u> ornate with simple features.

台灣總統府是典型的歐洲文藝復興與巴洛克建築的<u>組合</u>，<u>結合</u>華麗與簡約的特色。 100導遊

風俗民情

▶ In southern Taiwan, people's ties to <u>rural folk culture</u> are strongest. Local gods are more fervently <u>worshipped</u>. Tainan, for instance, has a temple heritage <u>second to none</u>.

南台灣人與民俗文化的連結是最強的，當地的神明被熱烈崇拜。例如台南，寺廟的文化首屈一指。 **100導遊**

▶ <u>Fireworks</u> and <u>firecrackers</u> are often used in Chinese communities to <u>symbolize</u> greeting good fortunes and scaring away evils.

煙火和鞭炮常用於華人社會中，來象徵迎接好運以及將晦氣嚇跑。 **99導遊**

▶ It is a <u>custom</u> for some Taiwanese to eat a bowl of long noodles on New Year's Eve. They feel that doing so will <u>increase</u> their chances of living long lives.

在台灣除夕吃碗長壽麵是項習俗。台灣人覺得如此一來能夠延年益壽。 **98導遊**

夜市 / 小吃 / 特產

▶ Pineapple cakes and local teas are some of the most popular <u>souvenirs</u> of Taiwan.

鳳梨酥和當地的茶葉是台灣最受歡迎的<u>紀念品</u>。 102領隊

▶ Taiwan Mountain Tea and Red Sprout Mountain Tea are <u>indigenous</u> sub-species of the island. They were discovered in Taiwan in the 17th century.

台灣高山茶和紅芽高山茶是島上<u>土生土長</u>的品種。他們於17世紀時在台灣被發現。 102領隊

▶ Tourists enjoy visiting night markets around the island to taste <u>authentic local snacks</u>.

遊客喜歡在島上到處參訪夜市，嚐嚐真正<u>道地的</u> 當地小吃。 99導遊

▶ Many foreigners who had visited Taiwan remembered the <u>throngs</u> of people packed into night markets and aromas floating through the air.

許多拜訪台灣的外國人都記得人<u>群</u>湧進夜市，以及香氣飄在空中。 100導遊

▶ The <u>highlight</u> of our trip to Southern Taiwan was A Taste of Tainan where we had a lot of delicious food.

南台灣之旅的<u>亮點</u>就是台南小吃，我們在那裡吃了很多美食。 101導遊

▶ Night markets in Taiwan have become <u>popular</u> <u>tourist destinations</u>. They are great places to shop for bargains and eat typical Taiwanese food.

台灣的夜市已經成為<u>受歡迎的</u> 觀光景點。他們是買便宜貨和吃傳統台灣料理的好地方。 101導遊

motorcar in the early 20th century. Railway companies in Europe and the United States used streamlined train 933 for high-speed services with an average speed of up to 130 km/h (80 mph) and a top speed of more than 16 00 mph). The first high-speed train was the Italian ETR 200 that in July 1939 went from Milan to Florence at 16 ith a top speed of 203 km/h. With this service, these trains were able to compete with the upcoming airplanes. he Odakyu Electric Railway in Greater Tokyo launched its Romancecar 3000 SSE. This set a world record fo gauge trains at 145 km/h (90 mph), giving Japanese designers confidence that they could safely build even fast standard gauge. Desperate for transport solutions due to overloaded trains between Tokyo and Osaka, the idea eed rail was born in Japan. There is no globally accepted standard separating high-speed rail from convention s; however, a number of widely accepted variables have been acknowledged by the industry in recent year ly, high-speed rail is defined as having a top speed in regular use of over 200 km/h (125 mph). A tour manager h al duties to perform to run a tour smoothly and successfully. For instance, the tour manager should always be th up every morning in order to make sure each team member is ready before the bus leaves for the next scenic sp

13. 活動盛事

ns, such as stolen passports, physical ailments and medical emergencies. Most importantly, the tour manager mu group members home safe and sound at the end of the journey and get ready for the next trip. Recently, a ne tourism, or what is called 'alternative tourism', has emerged and become more and more popular among peop l tired of the same old holidays and hope to gain real or authentic experiences from traveling. This new kind takes the form of individual custom-made or independent holidays that take people to remote and exot tions, and cater to their different needs and interests. These holidays are basically designed and arranged at l level. They often have different themes and offer a variety for people to choose from. As the market for this ne tourism has expanded greatly, newer topics and programs will also appear as long as people begin to devel nterests and needs in the future. But what exactly can people get out of alternative tourism? For ecology-mind they can go whale-watching or take a conservation trip to help restore the damaged coastline. For people who li re and outdoor activities, the choices could range from mountain climbing, scuba diving, windsurfing, white-wat to cycling in the mountains and deserts. For people who simply like to relax and gain a peace of mind, they c week at spa and health resorts to relax and de-stress, or take yoga and meditation lessons at country retreats for people who are fond of culture and heritage, they can visit museums and art galleries in New York, take d break at the Edinburgh International Festival, or tour around France to visit historic castles. Other progra lternative tourism include holidays that are taken for educational, artistic or religious purposes. These conta g English on a four-week trip to Australia, learning survival skills in the jungles, learning how to paint or hand uring a few days' holiday, and go on a pilgrimage to holy places and sites. The lists to these different kinds ns are

舉辦活動，像是舉辦遊行、運動會、各類展覽等等，可以説是
最常出現的考題之一，hold / host兩個單字的用法絕對不能忘記！

Railw average speed of up to 130 km/h (80 mph) and a top speed of more than 160 km/h (100 mph). The first high-spe as the Italian ETR 200 that in July 1939 went from Milan to Florence at 165 km/h, with a top speed of 203 km is service, these trains were able to compete with the upcoming airplanes. In 1957, the Odakyu Electric Railway Tokyo launched its Romancecar 3000 SSE. This set a world record for narrow gauge trains at 145 km/h (90 mph Japanese designers confidence that they could safely build even faster trains at standard gauge. Desperate

13. 活動盛事

host 主辦（帶有主辦人的意思）

hold 舉行、舉辦

take place、be held 發生、被舉辦

participate in 參加

popular 受歡迎的

popularity 歡迎

Olympics 奧運

Deaflympics 聽障奧運

Paralympic 殘障奧運

promote 行銷推廣

▶ An open-minded city, Taipei <u>hosted</u> Asia's first Gay Pride parade which has now become an annual autumn event.

身為一座心胸開放的都市，台北<u>主辦</u>亞洲第一屆同志遊行，並且成為每年於秋天所舉辦的活動。 `100導遊`

★補充：舉辦活動的兩個常見單字

① host 主辦（帶有主辦人的意思）

`例句` Rio will <u>host</u> the 2016 Summer Olympic Games.

　　 <u>里約</u>將<u>主辦</u>2016年夏季奧運。

② hold 舉行、舉辦

`例句` The Olympic Games are <u>held</u> every four years.

　　 奧運每4年<u>舉辦</u>一次。

`例句` The first Taipei Lantern Festival was <u>held</u> in 1990. Due to the event's huge popularity, the festival has been expanded every year.

　　 第一屆的台北燈籠節於1990年<u>舉行</u>。而因為這場活動受到極大的歡迎，慶祝活動一年比一年盛大。 `98導遊`

⚠ 重點：hold an event 舉辦活動，而此處活動名稱當主詞，故為被動式，was held 過去被舉辦；has been expanded 每年一直被擴張。

▶ The World Games of 2009 will <u>take place</u> in Kaohsiung, Taiwan, from July 16th to July 26th, 2009. The games will <u>feature</u> sports that are not contested in the Olympic Games.

2009年的世界運動大會將從7月16日至7月26日於台灣高雄<u>舉辦</u>。是<u>以</u>奧運未舉辦的比賽項<u>目為特色</u>。 98導遊

⚠ 重點：某事件take place = be held 發生、被舉辦，若是主辦單位為主詞，則可換成 Kaohsiung will host the World Games of 2009。

▶ A total of 3,965 <u>athletes</u> from 81 countries will compete in the 21st Summer Deaflympics to be <u>hosted</u> by Taipei City from September 5 to September 15 this year.

來自81個國家，總共3,965位<u>運動員</u>將於第21屆夏日聽障奧林匹克運動會一同競技，此次將由台北市於今年9月5日至9月15日<u>舉辦</u>。 98導遊

▶ Expo 2010 <u>will be held</u> in Shanghai, China from May 1 to October 31, 2010.

2010年的世界博覽會將在2010年5月1日到10月31日於中國上海舉行。 99領隊

▶ Millions of people are expected to <u>participate in</u> the 2010 Taipei International Flora Expo.

數百萬人期待<u>參加</u>2010年的台北國際花卉博覽會。 99領隊

▶ Starting in 2005, the Taipei City Government <u>began holding</u> its annual international Beef Noodle Soup Festival to <u>promote</u> the local favorite to visitors.

從2005年開始，台北市政府<u>開始舉辦</u>年度國際牛肉麵節以<u>推廣</u>本地的美食給觀光客。 98導遊

★補充：promote 推銷（動詞）為必考單字

例句 The company is <u>promoting</u> the new products now, so you can buy one and get the second one free.

公司現在正在<u>推廣</u>新產品，所以你可享買一送一的優惠。 98領隊

例句 To increase sales of products, many companies spend huge sums of money on <u>promotion</u> campaigns.

為了增加商品的銷售，很多公司花了大筆的金錢在<u>促銷</u>活動上。

98導遊

motorcar in the early 20th century. Railway companies in Europe and the United States used streamlined tra
933 for high-speed services with an average speed of up to 130 km/h (80 mph) and a top speed of more than 1
00 mph). The first high-speed train was the Italian ETR 200 that in July 1939 went from Milan to Florence at 1
with a top speed of 203 km/h. With this service, these trains were able to compete with the upcoming airplanes.
he Odakyu Electric Railway in Greater Tokyo launched its Romancecar 3000 SSE. This set a world record
gauge trains at 145 km/h (90 mph), giving Japanese designers confidence that they could safely build even fas
t standard gauge. Desperate for transport solutions due to overloaded trains between Tokyo and Osaka, the idea
eed rail was born in Japan. There is no globally accepted standard separating high-speed rail from convention
ds; however, a number of widely accepted variables have been acknowledged by the industry in recent yea
lly, high-speed rail is defined as having a top speed in regular use of over 200 km/h (125 mph). A tour manager h
ual duties to perform to run a tour smoothly and successfully. For instance, the tour manager should always be
e up every morning in order to make sure each team member is ready before the bus leaves for the next scenic s

14. 人格 / 個性

ns, such as stolen passports, physical ailments and medical emergencies. Most importantly, the tour manager m
e group members home safe and sound at the end of the journey and get ready for the next trip. Recently, a n
tourism, or what is called 'alternative tourism', has emerged and become more and more popular among peo
el tired of the same old holidays and hope to gain real or authentic experiences from traveling. This new kind
n takes the form of individual custom-made or independent holidays that take people to remote and exo
tions, and cater to their different needs and interests. These holidays are basically designed and arranged a
al level. They often have different themes and offer a variety for people to choose from. As the market for this n
f tourism has expanded greatly, newer topics and programs will also appear as long as people begin to devel
interests and needs in the future. But what exactly can people get out of alternative tourism? For ecology-mind
, they can go whale-watching or take a conservation trip to help restore the damaged coastline. For people who l
ure and outdoor activities, the choices could range from mountain climbing, scuba diving, windsurfing, white-wa
to cycling in the mountains and deserts. For people who simply like to relax and gain a peace of mind, they
a week at spa and health resorts to relax and de-stress, or take yoga and meditation lessons at country retreats
For people who are fond of culture and heritage, they can visit museums and art galleries in New York, tak
nd break at the Edinburgh International Festival, or tour around France to visit historic castles. Other progra
alternative tourism include holidays that are taken for educational, artistic or religious purposes. These cont
g English on a four-week trip to Australia, learning survival skills in the jungles, learning how to paint or han
uring a few days' holiday, and go on a pilgrimage to holy places and sites. The lists to these different kinds
ms are   nce of n
ys sign   ng faces
n, but   乍看之下，可能會覺得此分類和領隊導遊考題似乎沒有關係，   m of m
ortatio   但形容人的個性、行為等等的各類形容詞，經常出現於考題中。   e early 2
y. Railwa   eed servi
n average speed of up to 130 km/h (80 mph) and a top speed of more than 160 km/h (100 mph). The first high-sp
was the Italian ETR 200 that in July 1939 went from Milan to Florence at 165 km/h, with a top speed of 203 km
his service, these trains were able to compete with the upcoming airplanes. In 1957, the Odakyu Electric Railway
r Tokyo launched its Romancecar 3000 SSE. This set a world record for narrow gauge trains at 145 km/h (90 m
Japanese designers confidence that they could safely build even faster trains at standard gauge. Desperate

sunny 陽光性格的	blunt 遲鈍的
outgoing 外向的	reluctant 不願意的
shy 害羞的	open-minded 開放心胸的
humble、modest 謙虛的	witty 機智的
down-to-earth 樸實的	appreciation 鑑賞力
mature 成熟的	eccentric 怪異的
childish 幼稚的	clumsy 笨手笨腳的
disciplined 有紀律的	courteous、well-mannered、polite 禮貌的
considerate 體貼的	
thoughtful 細心的	discourteous、ill-mannered、impolite 沒禮貌的
sensitive 敏感的	

▶ People love to <u>socialize</u>, and Facebook makes it easier. The shy become more <u>outgoing</u> online.

人們喜歡<u>社交</u>，而臉書讓此更容易。害羞的人在網路上變得更外向。 `101導遊`

▶ The local tour guide has a <u>sunny personality</u>. Everybody likes him.

這位當地的導遊有著<u>陽光開朗的</u> 性格。每個人都喜歡他。 `101導遊`

★補充：描述天氣的形容詞

windy 風大的；stormy 暴風雨的；sunny 陽光的；cloudy 陰天的。

▶ As children grow and mature, they will leave behind <u>childish</u> pursuits, and no longer be so selfish and undisciplined as they used to be.

當小孩長大變成熟，他們將會把<u>幼稚</u>的行為拋下，且不再和以前一樣自私且沒有紀律。 99導遊

▶ <u>Considerate</u> people are sensitive to others' wants and feelings.

<u>體貼的人</u>通常容易察覺他人的需求以及感覺。 99導遊

▶ Kenneth is <u>reluctant</u> to <u>confide in</u> others, because he fears that the information he reveals will be used maliciously against him.

肯尼斯<u>不願意</u>向他人<u>敞開心胸</u>，因為他怕他所吐露的心聲會被惡意地用來對付他自己。 99導遊

▶ People who have a great sense of <u>humor</u> are often very popular, because they are usually intelligent, <u>open-minded</u>, and <u>witty</u>.

非常有<u>幽默感</u>的人通常很受歡迎，因為他們通常是聰明、<u>開放心胸</u>以及<u>機智</u>的。 99導遊

▶ A <u>humble</u> person is usually welcomed by everyone, because he never <u>irritates</u> people.

一個<u>謙虛的人</u>通常受到每個人的歡迎，因為這樣的人從不<u>激怒</u>其他人。 99導遊

▶ Elaine Hadley has many <u>hobbies</u>, such as horse-back riding, dancing, and playing with animals.

依蓮‧海德力有許多<u>嗜好</u>，像是騎馬、跳舞以及與動物們一起玩。 99導遊

▶ Sarah, who often <u>attends</u> symphony concerts, has a great <u>appreciation</u> for music.

那位常常<u>參加</u>交響樂會的莎拉，對於音樂有極高的<u>鑑賞力</u>。 99導遊

▶ The book is about a very <u>clumsy</u> boy who always breaks things.

這本書是關於一名<u>笨手笨腳的男生</u>，他總是打破東西。 `99導遊`

▶ Professor Nelson, who is rather strange, displays some <u>eccentric</u> behavior from time to time.

尼爾森教授是一個奇怪的人，有時會表現出<u>怪異的</u>行為。 `99導遊`

15. 健康

時差、減重、維持身體健康是最常考的三大健康命題。此類別比較不會出現艱澀難懂的單字，多半能以前後文推出答案，但首先要掌握相關單字。

15. 健康

關鍵單字

gain weight、put on weight 增重

maintain 維持

fitness 體態

diet 節食

exercise 運動

obesity 肥胖

overweight 過胖

body clock 生理時鐘

jet lag 時差

develop a new symptom 出現新症狀

contagious disease 接觸傳染病

cure 治療

paralyzed 癱瘓的

unconscious 無意識的（昏迷）

conscious 有意識的

subconscious 潛意識的

miracle 奇蹟

hazardous 有害的

blood sugar 血糖

diabetes 糖尿病

getting in shape、lose weight、lost pounds 減重

chronic health condition 慢性疾病的情形

嚴選佳句

▶ Many people have <u>put on some pounds</u> during the New Year vacation.

於新年假期期間，許多人<u>體重增加不少磅</u>。 `98領隊`

▶ Please don't order so much food! I have been <u>putting on weight</u> for the last two months.

拜託別點太多食物！這兩個月我已經開始<u>變胖</u>了。 `100領隊`

▶ Some families have children in chronic health conditions. At times, the pressure may be overwhelming to every individual in the family and the challenges can affect the quality of family life.

有些家庭的孩子有慢性疾病的情形。有時候壓力對於每一個家庭份子來說，有如排山倒海而來，而挑戰也會影響家庭生活的品質。 99導遊

▶ Christopher Reeve was paralyzed from the neck down and confined to a wheelchair, after the tragic accident.

在一場悲劇性的意外之後，克里斯多福‧李維從頸部以下都癱瘓了，並且得坐在輪椅上。 99導遊

▶ Shelly has adhered to a low-fat dlet for over two months and succeeded in losing 12 pounds.

雪莉已經遵循低卡飲食兩個多月，並且成功瘦下12磅。 102領隊

▶ Diabetes is a chronic disease whlch is difficult to cure. Management concentrates on keeping blood sugar levels as close to normal as possible without presenting undue patient danger.

糖尿病是一種慢性疾病且難以治癒。日常管理上需注意血糖高低需接近正常值，不要讓病人有過度危險的狀況發生。 100導遊

▶ Caused by the disruption of our "body clock," jet lag can be a big problem for most travelers in the first few days after they have arrived at their destination.

由於「生理時鐘」的混亂，時差對於大多數的旅遊者而言，在抵達目的地的前幾天會是一大問題。 98導遊

▶ I seem to have a <u>fever</u>. May I have a <u>thermometer</u> to take my temperature?

我好像<u>發燒</u>了。可以給我<u>溫度計</u>來量溫度嗎？ 100導遊

▶ <u>Obesity</u> has become a very serious problem in the modern world. It's estimated that there are more than 1 billion <u>overweight</u> adults globally.

<u>肥胖</u>已經成為現代世界很嚴重的問題。預估全球有超過10億成人<u>過重</u>。 99領隊

▶ Many people have made "<u>getting in shape</u>" one of their new year <u>resolutions</u>.

很多人的新年新<u>願望</u>都希望可以「<u>減肥</u>」。 102領隊

▶ The chemicals in these cleaning products can be <u>hazardous</u> to our health.

清潔用品中的化學物質對我們的健康可能是<u>有害的</u>。 102領隊

▶ The doctor thought she could never walk. But now she can not only walk but run as well. It is really a <u>miracle</u>.

醫生原本以為她不可能再走路了。但是她現在不但可以走，還能跑。這真是<u>奇蹟</u>。 98導遊

▶ As a result of the accident, Shirley was <u>unconscious</u> for three weeks before gradually <u>recovered</u>.

這次意外的結果，雪麗在逐漸<u>恢復</u>之前<u>昏迷</u>了3個星期。 99導遊

▶ Scientists have found a <u>cure</u> for the rare contagious disease, and some patients now have the hope of <u>recovery</u>.

科學家已經發現罕見接觸性疾病的<u>療法</u>，現在一些病人對於<u>治癒</u>懷抱希望。 99導遊

▶ Scarlet fever is a/an <u>contagious</u> disease, which is transferable from one person to another.

猩紅熱是一種<u>接觸傳染性的</u>疾病，是經由人與人接觸傳染。 99導遊

▶ Middle-aged smokers are far more likely than nonsmokers to <u>develop</u> dementia later in life, and heavy smokers are at more than double the risk, according to a new study.

根據一項新研究，中年吸菸的人比不吸菸的人在往後的日子裡更容易<u>得</u>到失智症，且有菸癮的人有超過2倍以上的風險。 100導遊

▶ To <u>maintain</u> health and fitness, we need proper <u>diet</u> and exercise.

為了<u>維持</u>健康和體態，我們需要適量的<u>節食</u>和運動。 101導遊

motorcar in the early 20th century. Railway companies in Europe and the United States used streamlined tra
933 for high-speed services with an average speed of up to 130 km/h (80 mph) and a top speed of more than 1
100 mph). The first high-speed train was the Italian ETR 200 that in July 1939 went from Milan to Florence at 1
with a top speed of 203 km/h. With this service, these trains were able to compete with the upcoming airplanes.
he Odakyu Electric Railway in Greater Tokyo launched its Romancecar 3000 SSE. This set a world record
gauge trains at 145 km/h (90 mph), giving Japanese designers confidence that they could safely build even fas
t standard gauge. Desperate for transport solutions due to overloaded trains between Tokyo and Osaka, the idea
eed rail was born in Japan. There is no globally accepted standard separating high-speed rail from conventio
ds; however, a number of widely accepted variables have been acknowledged by the industry in recent yea
lly, high-speed rail is defined as having a top speed in regular use of over 200 km/h (125 mph). A tour manager l
ual duties to perform to run a tour smoothly and successfully. For instance, the tour manager should always be
e up every morning in order to make sure each team member is ready before the bus leaves for the next scenic s

16. 職場 / 學校

ns, such as stolen passports, physical ailments and medical emergencies. Most importantly, the tour manager m
e group members home safe and sound at the end of the journey and get ready for the next trip. Recently, a n
f tourism, or what is called 'alternative tourism', has emerged and become more and more popular among peo
el tired of the same old holidays and hope to gain real or authentic experiences from traveling. This new kind
n takes the form of individual custom-made or independent holidays that take people to remote and exo
tions, and cater to their different needs and interests. These holidays are basically designed and arranged a
al level. They often have different themes and offer a variety for people to choose from. As the market for this n
f tourism has expanded greatly, newer topics and programs will also appear as long as people begin to devel
interests and needs in the future. But what exactly can people get out of alternative tourism? For ecology-min
, they can go whale-watching or take a conservation trip to help restore the damaged coastline. For people who l
ure and outdoor activities, the choices could range from mountain climbing, scuba diving, windsurfing, white-wa
to cycling in the mountains and deserts. For people who simply like to relax and gain a peace of mind, they
a week at spa and health resorts to relax and de-stress, or take yoga and meditation lessons at country retreats
For people who are fond of culture and heritage, they can visit museums and art galleries in New York, tak
d break at the Edinburgh International Festival, or tour around France to visit historic castles. Other progra
alternative tourism include holidays that are taken for educational, artistic or religious purposes. These cont

人與人最常互動的場合，莫過於學校與職場，因此領隊導遊英文經常著墨於職場、學校上的點點滴滴，包含面試、加薪、升遷等等，都是相當生活化且實用的考題。

average speed of up to 130 km/h (80 mph) and a top speed of more than 160 km/h (100 mph). The first high-sp
as the Italian ETR 200 that in July 1939 went from Milan to Florence at 165 km/h, with a top speed of 203 km
his service, these trains were able to compete with the upcoming airplanes. In 1957, the Odakyu Electric Railway
Tokyo launched its Romancecar 3000 SSE. This set a world record for narrow gauge trains at 145 km/h (90 m
Japanese designers confidence that they could safely build even faster trains at standard gauge. Desperate

關鍵單字

agenda 議程	coordination 協調
mock interview 模擬的面試	crew 工作人員
personnel manager 人事主管	embarrassing 使人尷尬的，指事物
preside over 主持	embarrassed 感到尷尬的
absent 缺席的	work as a team 團體工作
present 出席的	work independently 獨立工作
salesperson 業務	survey 調查
qualified 資格	jeopardize 危害
on behalf of 代表	prestigious 有名氣的
filed a protest 發起抗議	competitive 競爭的
unemployed 失業的	requirement 需求
employee 員工	initiative 倡議
clock in 打卡	expel 開除
demanding 苛求的	sign up 報名登記
assign 分配、分派	faculty 教職員
consider 考慮	in the dark 一無所知
applicant 申請者	remind 提醒
submit 提交	borrow from 從某處借來
submit a plan 提出一項計畫	return 歸還
disjointed 脫節鬆散的、支離破碎的	highlight 重點

▶ According to the meeting <u>agenda</u>, three more topics are to be discussed this afternoon.

根據會議<u>議程</u>，這個下午還有3個議題要被討論。 101導遊

▶ Beatrix's friend had given her a <u>mock</u> interview before she actually went to meet the <u>personnel manager</u> of the company she was applying to.

貝翠絲的朋友給她一個<u>模擬的</u>面試，在她真的要和所申請工作公司的<u>人事主管</u>面試之前。 100導遊

▶ It has been my honor and pleasure to work with him for more than 10 years. His insight and analysis are always <u>impressive</u>.

能與他共事超過10年以上是我的榮幸。他的洞見和分析總是<u>令人印象深刻</u>。 101導遊

▶ Since the president of the company is <u>absent</u>, the general manager will <u>preside</u> over the meeting.

既然公司總裁<u>缺席</u>，總經理將會<u>主持</u>這場會議。 99導遊

▶ Cathy is an <u>outgoing</u> and successful <u>salesperson</u>, but her <u>background</u> is in web design.

凱西是很<u>活潑</u>成功的<u>業務</u>，但她的<u>出身背景</u>是網頁設計。 99導遊

▶ Upon <u>agreeing</u> to the plan, the organizers are to <u>set out the procedures</u>.

一旦<u>同意</u>計畫，負責人員就開始<u>設定步驟</u>。 102領隊

▶ As Tim has no experience at all, I <u>doubt</u> he is <u>qualified</u> for this job.

因為提姆沒有任何經驗，我<u>懷疑</u>他是否<u>有資格</u>勝任這份工作。 102領隊

▶ The Union has <u>filed a protest</u> <u>on behalf of</u> the terminated workers.

公會已經代表被資遣的工人發起抗議。 `102領隊`

▶ The manager lacked <u>coordination</u> and communication skills; likewise, his crew was altogether <u>disjointed</u>.

這名經理缺乏<u>統整</u>以及溝通技巧，同樣地，他的人員也都很<u>散亂</u>。 `102領隊`

▶ Having been <u>unemployed</u> for almost one year, Henry has little chance of getting a job.

因為亨利已經<u>失業</u>幾乎一年了，他找到工作的機會很小。 `101領隊`

▶ All the <u>employees</u> have to use an electronic card to <u>clock in</u> when they arrive for work.

當抵達辦公室時，所有的<u>員工</u>都必須使用電子卡來<u>打卡</u>。 `101領隊`

▶ The non-smoking policy will <u>apply</u> to any person working for the company <u>regardless</u> of their status or position.

禁菸政策將<u>適用</u>於任何在公司工作的人，<u>不管</u>其地位或職位。 `101領隊`

> ⚠ 重點：regardless 無論如何；regarding 「關於某事」的3種用法：「regarding something」、「with regard to something」、「as regards something」。

▶ I would like to express our gratitude to you <u>on behalf of</u> my company.

我想要<u>代表</u>我的公司向你表達感謝之意。 `101領隊`

▶ Those wishing to be considered for <u>paid leave</u> should put their requests in as soon as possible.

想要考慮<u>有薪假</u>的人應該盡快提出申請。 `101領隊`

▶ Whoever is first to arrive in the office is responsible for checking the voice mail.

不論是誰第一個進到辦公室，要負責檢查語音信箱。 (101領隊)

▶ My boss is very demanding; he keeps asking us to complete assigned tasks within the limited time span.

我的老闆很嚴苛，他一直要求我們在有限的時間內完成指定任務。 (98導遊)

▶ We all felt embarrassed when the manager got drunk.

當經理喝醉時，我們都感到很不好意思。 (100領隊)

▶ If you want to work in tourism, you need to know how to work as part of a team. But sometimes, you also need to know how to work independently.

如果你想要在旅遊業工作，你需要知道如何和團體工作。但有時候你也需要知道如何獨立作業。 (99領隊)

▶ John has to submit the annual report to the manager before this Friday; otherwlse, he wlll be ln trouble.

約翰必須在這週五之前提交年度報告給經理，不然他就完蛋了。 (99領隊)

▶ Due to his lack of experience, the applicant was not considered for the job.

由於他的經驗不足，這名申請者不被考慮錄取這份工作。 (101領隊)

▶ The company had the market surveyed by a nationally-known research firm.

這間公司請了全國知名的研究公司來做市場調查。 (101領隊)

▶ Before the applicant left, the interviewer asked him for a current contact number so that he could be reached if he was given the job.

在應徵者離開之前，面試人員向他要聯絡電話，若是錄取便得以聯絡。 (101領隊)

▶ May I remind you not to <u>jeopardize</u> your success on an important test by watching a movie instead of studying hard.

讓我提醒你不要因為看電影而沒有用功唸書，<u>危害</u>了你重要考試的好表現。

`100導遊`

▶ Most <u>prestigious</u> private schools are highly <u>competitive</u> – that is, they have stiffer admissions <u>requirements</u>.

大部分<u>有名氣的</u>私立學校都很<u>競爭</u>，也就是他們有比較嚴格的入學<u>條件</u>。

`100導遊`

▶ Katherine was <u>reminded</u> to <u>return</u> the book by next Monday, which she <u>borrowed</u> from the school library three months ago.

凱薩琳被<u>提醒</u>下週一<u>還</u>書，那是她3個月前從學校圖書館<u>借</u>的。 `99導遊`

▶ The students were completely <u>in the dark</u> about their graduation trip because the school wanted it to be a surprise.

學生對於畢業旅行<u>一無所知</u>，因為學校希望這是一個驚喜。 `100導遊`

> ⚠ 重點：用直譯來看in the dark為在黑暗中，也就是什麼都看不到、不清楚的意思。
> 另外have no clue也可代表一無所知的意思。

▶ One of the most important parts of these activities is for students to share the <u>highlights</u> of a group discussion with the rest of the class.

這些活動最重要的部分之一就是讓學生和班上分享團體討論的<u>重點</u>。 `102領隊`

▶ A group of young students has <u>taken the initiative</u> through <u>social media</u> to organize a rally against the austerity plans.

一群年輕學生透過<u>社群媒體</u><u>發動</u>對抗撙節計畫。 `102領隊`

▶ <u>Stay calm</u> and clear-minded. I'm sure you'll have no problem <u>passing</u> the exam.

保持冷靜和清晰的思路。我敢保證你可以沒有問題地通過考試。 `102領隊`

> ⚠ 重點：have no problem + V-ing 做某事沒有問題；have problems + V-ing 做某事有問題 / 困難 = have trouble / difficulty + V-ing。

▶ The school boys <u>stopped</u> bullying the stray dog when their teacher went up to them.

當他們的老師走向他們時，這些男學生停止欺負流浪狗。 `101領隊`

> ⚠ 重點：stop + V-ing表示停止做某事；stop to V表示停下手邊之事，去做某事。

▶ Tom was <u>expelled</u> from his school for stealing and cheating on the exams.

湯姆被學校開除是因為偷竊以及考試作弊。 `99領隊`

▶ He runs away with the idea, and the other <u>faculty members</u> do not agree.

他倉促地說出想法，而其他教職員不同意。 `100領隊`

▶ Bonnie <u>signed up</u> for dancing classes in the Extension Program.

邦妮報名登記了推廣教育的舞蹈課。 `100領隊`

國家圖書館出版品預行編目資料

完全命中！領隊導遊英文考前衝刺 / 陳若慈著
--初版--臺北市：瑞蘭國際, 2014.02
176面；17 x 23公分--（繽紛外語系列；31）
ISBN：978-986-5953-64-5（平裝）
1.英語 2.讀本

805.18   103001113

■ 繽紛外語系列 31

完全命中

作者｜陳若慈‧責任編輯｜葉仲芸‧校對｜陳若慈、葉仲芸、王愿琦

封面、版型設計、內文排版｜余佳憓‧印務｜王彥萍

董事長｜張暖彗‧社長兼總編輯｜王愿琦‧副總編輯｜呂依臻
主編｜王彥萍、葉仲芸‧編輯｜陳秋汝‧美術編輯｜余佳憓
業務部主任｜楊米琪‧業務部助理｜林湲洵

出版社｜瑞蘭國際有限公司‧地址｜台北市大安區安和路一段104號7樓之1
電話｜(02)2700-4625‧傳真｜(02)2700-4622‧訂購專線｜(02)2700-4625
劃撥帳號｜19914152 瑞蘭國際有限公司‧瑞蘭網路書城｜www.genki-japan.com.tw

總經銷｜聯合發行股份有限公司‧電話｜(02)2917-8022、2917-8042
傳真｜(02)2915-6275、2915-7212‧印刷｜宗祐印刷有限公司
出版日期｜2014年02月初版1刷‧定價｜250元‧ISBN｜978-986-5953-64-5

aircraft、plane	飛機
airplane	飛機、航空公司
airport security rules	機場安全規定
airport	機場
aisle seat	靠走道的座位
aliens	外國人
alternative	其他的選擇
amazing	令人驚豔的
amenities	設施

a must-see for visitors	必遊景點
a train / bus route	火車 / 公車路線
absent	缺席的
accommodation	住宿
adventure	冒險
affordable	買得起的
agenda	議程
agreement	協議
ahead	事先

A

applicant	申請者
appreciate	欣賞
appreciation	鑑賞力
appropriate / inappropriate	合宜的／不合宜的
approval	同意
arrival desk	入境櫃台
arrival time	到達時間
arrive	(人、飛機) 到達
assign	分配、分派

A

auction	拍賣
authentic	道地的
available	可得到的

B

bachelor	單身漢
baggage allowance	行李限額
baggage claim	行李領取中心
baggage claim tag	行李存根

B

bail out	保釋、紓困
ban	禁止
bank note	鈔票
bargain	好價錢
be categorized	被分類
be graded	被評分
be ranked	被排名
be steeped in	充滿著、沉浸於
bed down	下榻

B

bill	法案
blood sugar	血糖
blunt	遲鈍的
boarding gate	登機門
boarding pass	登機證
body clock	生理時鐘
booming growth	蓬勃成長
boost the economy	振興經濟
boutique	精品店

B

bowl	碗
breath-taking	令人屏息的
bridal tour、honeymoon	蜜月旅行
bride	新娘
brochure	小冊子
budget airline、low-cost airline	廉價航空
budget	預算、控制預算
business class	商務艙

C

cabin crew	機組人員
capital	首都
captain	機長
carry	攜帶
carry-on luggage / baggage	隨身行李
cascade	疊層成瀑布落下
cash	現金
casino	賭場
cater	迎合、承辦伙食

caution	警告
cellphone、mobile phone	手機
census	人口普查
challenge	挑戰
character	內在的特質
charge	費用、收費
charming	迷人的
chart	圖表
charter bus	遊覽車

checked baggage	託運行李
check-in desk	辦理登機手續的櫃台
check-in	登記住房
check-in	辦理登機手續
check-out	結帳、退房
registration form	登記表
childish	幼稚的
chronic health condition	慢性疾病的情形
clear customs	清關、通關

C

clock in	打卡
clumsy	笨手笨腳的
collection	收藏品
committed	致力於
compensate	補償
compete with	比得上
competitive	競爭的
complimentary	免費
compulsory	義務的

C

concert hall	音樂廳
concierge service	管家服務
concierge	旅館服務台人員
confirm flight	確認班機
confirm	確認
congress	立法機關
connecting flight	轉機班機
conscious	有意識的
consider	考慮

C

considerate	體貼的
contagious disease	接觸傳染病
contingency plan	備案
contrast	對比
coordination	協調
court	法院
courteous、well-mannered、polite	禮貌的
credit card	信用卡
crew	工作人員

C

cripple	嚴重毀壞或損害
cross-strait relations	兩岸關係
cruise	飛行、航行
cuisine	美食
cure	治療
currency exchange	換匯
custody	監護權
custom	風俗
customary	約定俗成的

D

deposit	訂金
destination	目的地
develop a new symptom	出現新症狀
diabetes	糖尿病
diet	節食
difference	不同之處
direct flight	直飛班機
disaster	災害、災難
disciplined	有紀律的

D

discourteous、ill-mannered、impolite	沒禮貌的
disembark flight	下飛機
disembarkation	下船、下飛機
disjointed	脫節鬆散的、支離破碎的
divert	轉向
divorce	離婚
domestic flight	國內航班
domestic	國內的
dos and don'ts	注意事項

D

down-to-earth	樸實的
draw attention to	引起對……的注意
dress code	穿衣法則
due to	因為
duty	職責

E

| eccentric | 怪異的 |
| ecology | 生態環境 |

E

economic recession	經濟蕭條
economic slowdown	經濟趨緩
economic trauma	經濟創傷
economy class	經濟艙
ecotourism	生態旅遊
eliminate	消滅
embarkation	乘船、搭飛機
embarrassed	感到尷尬的
embarrassing	使人尷尬的；指事物

E

employee	員工
enigma	謎
enigmatic	謎樣的
entitle	有……權力
entry permit	入境許可證
environmentally friendly	對生態環境無害的
equator	赤道
ethics	道德
examine、inspect	檢查

E

exchange rate	匯率
excursion	遠足
exercise	運動
exotic	異國風情的
expel	開除
expire	過期
expiry date	到期日
export	出口
express	快的、直達的、快車

F

facility	設施
faculty	教職員
familiarize with	熟悉
fare	（大眾運輸）票價
fascinate	使神魂顛倒
fasten	繫緊
feature	特色
fee	費用
file a complaint	投訴

F

file for divorce	提出離婚訴訟
final boarding call、final call	最後登機廣播
finance	財經
financial crisis	金融危機
fine	處以……罰金
firecrackers	鞭炮
fireworks	煙火
first class	頭等艙
first impression	第一印象

F

fitness	體能
flight attendant	空服員
flight safety	飛行安全
flight	班機
flourish	蓬勃發展
foreign currency	外幣
foreign	國外的、陌生的
foreigner	外國人
fraud	欺騙行為、詭計、騙局

F

fresh	新鮮的
front desk	櫃台

G

gain weight、put on weight	增重
gallery	藝廊
get off an airplane / a bus	下飛機／巴士
get on an airplane / a bus	上飛機／巴士
greet	問候

G

greetings	問候語
guest service	客戶服務
groom	新郎
guided tour	有導遊的遊覽

H

hand luggage / baggage	手提行李
handy	方便
have an affair with	與……有染

H

hazardous	有害的
headquarters	總部、總公司
heavy user	重度使用者
high season、peak season	旺季
highlight	亮點、重點
hiking	健行
historic site	歷史遺址
hold	舉行、舉辦
host	主辦

H

hotel clerk	飯店人員
humble、modest	謙虛的

I

identification	證件
immigrant	移民者
immigration officer	移民官
immigration	移民
imminent	逼近的、即將發生的

I

impact	影響、衝擊
impending	即將發生的、逼近的
import	進口
impose	徵（稅）
in advance	事先
inclement weather	惡劣的天氣
income	收入、所得
indifference	漠不關心
indigenous	本地的、土生土長的

I

inflation	通貨膨脹
infrastructure	公共建設
initiate	開始、發起
initiative	倡議
inquire	詢問
international flight	國際航班
international trade	國際貿易
island	島嶼
itinerary	旅程、路線、行程

J

jeopardize	危害
jet lag	時差
journey	旅程

K

known for、famous for	知名

light season	淡季
litter	亂扔廢棄物
lobby	旅館大廳
local snack	當地小吃
lodging	住宿
lose weight、lost pounds	減重
luggage、baggage	行李（不可數名詞）
luxurious	奢華的
luxury	奢侈品、奢華

land、touch down	降落
landscape	風景、景色
large denomination	大鈔
leave for、head to	前往某處
leave message	留話
legal interest	法定利息
legalize	合法化
leisurely	悠閒地
lift oneself out of poverty	讓某人脫貧

M

maintain	維持
make reservation	訂位、預約
Mandarin	中文
manner	態度、禮貌
map	地圖
marvelous scenery	絕美風光
mature	成熟的
meander	蜿蜒而流
metropolitan / urban area	都會區

M

metropolitan	大都市的
middle seat	中間的座位
miracle	奇蹟
mock interview	模擬面試
modern	現代的
momentum	勢力
museum	博物館

National Palace Museum	故宮博物院
necessary	需要的
necessity	必需品
newlywed	新婚夫婦
notion	概念、想法

obesity	肥胖
occasion	場合

O

old-fashioned	舊式的
Olympics	奧運
on behalf of	代表
open-minded	開放心胸的
operate	運作、運轉
outbreak	暴動
outdated、obsolete	過時的
outgoing	外向的
overweight	過胖

package holiday	套裝行程
panoramic	全景的
palace	皇宮
Paralympic	殘障奧運
paralyzed	癱瘓的
parlor	休息室、接待室
participate in	參加
passenger	乘客
passport control	護照審查管理處

passport	護照
path	小徑、小路
peak	山頂
perform	表演
personal belongings	隨身物品
personality	外在的性格
personnel manager	人事主管
personnel	人員
phenomenon	現象

P

precaution	預防
present	出席的
prestigious	有名氣的
pricey	昂貴的
prohibited items	違禁品
promote	行銷推廣
prosperity	興旺、繁榮

P

photogenic	上相的
physically impaired	殘障的
pick up	領取
plate	盤子
polite / impolite	禮貌的 / 不禮貌的
popular	受歡迎的
popularity	歡迎
population	人口
poverty	貧窮、貧困

Q

| qualified | 資格 |

R

reasonable	價格合理的
reception	接待處
reconfirm	再次確認
refrain	避免、忍住、抑制
refund	退款
reluctant	不願意的

R

rely on、depend on、count on	依靠、信賴
remarkably	明顯地、非常地
remind	提醒
replace	取代
require	需要、要求
requirement	需求
reservation	預訂
reserve a table	訂桌
reserve	預約、預訂

R

reserved	（被）保留的
resort	名勝
responsibility	責任
responsible for	對⋯⋯有責任
retreat	僻靜之處
revenue	稅收
reward	獎賞
rewarding	有價值的
room rate	房價

R

round-trip ticket	來回票
route	路線、路程
rural area	鄉村、郊區
rural folk culture	民俗文化
rural	鄉村的、農村的、田園的
rustic	鄉下的

S

safari	狩獵遠征

salesperson	業務
sample	品檔
satisfactory	令人滿意的、符合要求的
scenic waterfall	美景瀑布
search	搜查
seat belt	安全帶
secluded beach	隱密性海灘
secluded	隱蔽的、僻靜的
second to none	不亞於任何人、首屈一指

secure reservation	確保訂位／房
security check	安全檢查
seniors	長者、前輩、資深人士
sensitive	敏感的
serene	寧靜的
set meal	套餐
set route	固定的路線
shuttle service	接駁巴士服務
shy	害羞的

social manner	社交禮儀
souvenir	紀念品
specialty	招牌菜
spectacle	奇觀
spectacular	壯觀的、壯麗的
stale	不新鮮的
staple	主食
step out	踏出
steward	空少

sightseeing bus (boat)	觀光巴士（船）
sign up	報名登記
significant	有意義的、重要的
single ticket	單程票
sit back	放鬆休息
site	地點、場所、網站
small denomination	小鈔
smother	阻擋、阻礙
social isolation	社會隔離

S

stewardess	空姐
stopover	中途停留
stormy weather	暴風雨的天氣
stuff	物品、東西
subconscious	潛意識的
submit a plan	提出一項計畫
submit	提交
suite	套房
sunny	陽光性格的

S

surcharge	附加費用
surge	激增
survey	調查
symbol	符號
symbolize	象徵

T

table manner	餐桌禮儀
take [have, go for] a stroll	散步、漫步

throng	人群
tie the knot	結婚
today's special	今日特餐
tour guide	導遊
tour manager	領隊
tour	旅遊
Tourism Bureau	觀光旅遊局
tourism	觀光業
tourist destination / spots	觀光景點

take caution	注意
take message	幫……留話
take place	舉行、發生、被舉辦
tax rebate	退稅
taxi in	飛機在航道上滑行
telephone fraud	電話詐欺
temple	廟宇
thoughtful	細心的
thrilling	令人興奮的

T

tourist	觀光客
transaction	交易
transfer	轉機
transit	過境
transportation vehicles	交通工具
travel agent	旅行社
traveler's check / cheque	旅行支票
turbulence	亂流

U

unavailable	不可得的
unconscious	無意識的（昏迷）
unemployed	失業的
unnecessary	不需要的
unsatisfactory	不令人滿意的
urban	城市的、都會的
urge	催促、力勸

vacancy	空房、空位
vacant	空的
visa	簽證
visually impaired	視障的

| wander | 漫遊、閒逛 |
| wedding anniversary | 結婚周年 |

weigh luggage / baggage	行李過磅、行李秤重
welfare	福利
famous、renowned	有名的
window seat	靠窗的座位
wireless internet access	無線網路
withdraw	提領
within the law	合法
witty	機智的
wonders of the world	世界奇景

W

work as a team ...... 團體工作

work independently ...... 獨立工作

Z

zone ...... 地帶、地區

補充
單字

補充單字

補充單字

補充單字